Praise for Jon Fosse

"Jon Fosse is a major European writer."
—Karl Ove Knausgaard

"Fosse . . . has been compared to Ibsen and to Beckett, and it is easy to see his work as Ibsen stripped down to its emotional essentials. But it is much more. For one thing, it has a fierce poetic simplicity."
—*New York Times*

". . . an exploration of zones that are murky, dangerous, crucial, where craftsmanship and inspiration seek and repulse each other."
—*Le Monde*

"Fosse's pared down, circuitous, and rhythmic prose skillfully guides readers through past and present."
—*Publishers Weekly*

"He is undoubtedly one of the world's most important and versatile literary voices."
—*Irish Examiner*

"Norway's biggest cultural export."
—*Norwegian National Television (NRK)*

"The Beckett of the 21st Century."
—*Le Monde*

"There is something quietly dramatic about Fosse's meandering and rhythmic prose . . . which has a strangely mesmerising effect."
—*The Independent*

Other Books by Jon Fosse
in English Translation

Jon Fosse

TRILOGY

Translated from the Norwegian by May-Brit Akerholt

Introduction by Cecilie Seiness

DALKEY ARCHIVE PRESS

DALLAS, TX · ROCHESTER, NY

Originally published in Norwegian as *Andvake* (2007), *Olavs draumar* (2012), and *Kvldsvaevd* (2014) by Det Norske Samlaget. All three books were published together as *Trilogien* by Det Norske Samlaget in 2014.

Library of Congress Cataloging-in-Publication Data

Names: Fosse, Jon, 1959- author. | Akerholt, May-Brit, translator. | Fosse, Jon, 1959- Andvake. English. | Fosse, Jon, 1959- Olavs draumar. English. | Fosse, Jon, 1959- Kvldsvaevd. English.
Title: Trilogy / Jon Fosse ; translated by May-Brit Akerholt.
Other titles: Trilogien. English
Description: First Dalkey Archive edition. | Victoria, TX : Dalkey Archive Press, 2016. | "Originally published in Norwegian as Andvake (2007), Olavs draumar (2012), and Kvldsvaevd (2014) by Det Norske Samlaget. All three books were later published together as Trilogien by Det Norske Samlaget in 2014" — Verso title page.
Identifiers: LCCN 2016010910 | ISBN 9781628971392 (pbk.: alk. paper)
Subjects: LCSH: Fosse, Jon, 1959—Translations into English. | Unmarried couples—Fiction. | Homeless teenagers—Fiction. | Pregnant teenagers—Fiction. | Bergen (Norway)-Fiction. | GSAFD: Love stories. Classification: LCC PT8951.16.073 T7513 2016 | DDC 839.823/74-dc23 LC record available at https://lccn.loc.gov/2016010910
Partially funded by a grant by the Illinois Arts Council, a state agency.
This translation has been published with the financial support of NORLA (Norwegian Literature Abroad) foundation.
N NORLA
NORWEGIAN LITERATURE ABROAD

www.dalkeyarchive.com
Dallas, TX / Rochester, NY

An Itinerant Player in Life

"This author has been able, like few others, to carve out his own literary form. Echoes and resonances from the Bible and Christian visionary poetry are combined with poetic images and suspenseful elements in a way that allows the story of two people in love to open up onto the world and history."

These words are from the jury statement awarding Jon Fosse's *Trilogy* the Nordic Council Literature Prize in 2015. *Trilogy* consists of three short texts that came out years apart: *Andvake* in 2007, *Olavs draumar* in 2012, and *Kveldsvævd* in the spring of 2014 (translated here as *Wakefulness*, *Olav's Dreams*, and *Weariness*). Each is a good story on its own, but collected into a novel it is far more than the sum of its parts. Only as a trilogy did the book really find its audience; one critic in the Danish newspaper *Politiken* wrote that *Trilogy* "will still be read in five hundred years."

Wakefulness is a beautiful, disturbing story about a fiddler, Asle, and his love, Alida. The couple has had to leave their village and wander sleepless in the rain in Bjørgvin. In *Olav's Dreams*, we meet Asle on his way to get rings. In the last volume, *Weariness*, we learn through old Ales, Alida's daughter, what happened to the couple who sacrificed their conscience for love.

Trilogy, while less than 240 small book pages in Norwegian, is full of action, including murder, violence, and not least love. And the story of the fiddler and his love has traveled far since 2014. It can be found in book form in Russia, South Korea, Iceland, Portugal, Albania, France, and Germany; *Trilogy* is one of Fosse's books of fiction that have truly reached a large number of people.

On October 27, 2015, Jon Fosse stood on stage at the Harpa Concert Hall in Reykjavik and received the prestigious Nordic Council prize. He was happy and grateful. By this time Fosse had become a successful playwright; his plays were performed all over the world and he had already received a number of awards, but usually for drama or else his whole body of work. This time it was a fiction prize, and fiction was and is at least as important to Fosse as drama. The prize was the confirmation he needed in 2015, because he wanted to write more fiction. He was done with drama, at least for a while. *Trilogy* was his way back to where it all started.

The action in *Trilogy* takes place in Vestland, western Norway, on the water and in a boat, in a village and in the city of Bjørgvin, where the rain pours steadily down. Bergen, the largest city in western Norway, used to be known as Bjørgvin. Fosse is a "Vestlander," inextricably linked to western Norway—the mountains, the fjord, the sea, and the mentality and language there. He was born in the village of Strandebarm in Hardanger in 1959, and grew up there, about two hours from Bergen—a boy from a small farm, close to the fjord and the waves, far from the city and the nearest theater. He was interested neither in books nor in theater as a child, and instead was obsessed with playing the guitar: he practiced like a madman, day and night, and was a guitarist in a band that played at dances, but after a while he switched from guitar to keyboard. He started writing when he was quite young, inventing what he called a secret space of writing. This secret space was something completely different from school writing.

Norway has two written languages, Bokmål and Nynorsk. While Nynorsk is based on the vernacular and on Norwegian dialects, Bokmål is based on Danish. The majority of people in Norway write in Bokmål, but Nynorsk is strong in western Norway, except for in Bergen. In Hardanger and western Norway as a whole, Nynorsk is the natural first language; Fosse has always written in Nynorsk, anything else is unthinkable. He is an ardent proponent of Nynorsk and an unusually erudite user of the language. In many ways, western Norway stands in contrast to the capital, Oslo: fjords and mountains, dripping rain and Nynorsk, and also, traditionally strong Christian beliefs. In the village where Fosse grew up, there were both youth community centers and houses of prayer, both God and dances in bars. Pietism marked Fosse's upbringing as well, through the house of prayer, the church, and Sunday school for children. At sixteen, though, the rebellious young Fosse left the state church. Later, Fosse felt that, as he put it, writing was pushing him out of atheism; in 2013, he converted to Catholicism.

On that stage in Iceland, the Norwegian Prime Minister, Erna Solberg, was one of the first to congratulate the prize winner. She tried to make the award a victory for Bergen, western Norway's main city, where Fosse had lived for many years as well as her own hometown. Fosse refused: "No, I wouldn't say that. This is a prize for Vestland. Western Norway is the main area for Nynorsk *except* for Bergen. The dominant language there is Bokmål or Riksmål or Dano-Norwegian."

Even as a young man, Fosse thought of himself as a rural intellectual with artistic inclinations. When he left home to go to the academic high school in Øystese, he took his father's old typewriter with him, a Remington. In the autumn of 1979, Fosse moved to Bergen. He wanted to write. A short story competition in the student newspaper in Bergen is what really made the long-haired student think that writing was something he could do. Fosse won with the short story "He," about two silent men. With its repetitions, suggestions, and inner monologues it is already unmistakable Fosse, both in the writing style and in how it shows people behaving with one another. Fosse himself considers this story his debut. Not long after winning the student competition in 1983, his debut novel was published: *Raudt, svart* [*Red, Black*]. It is about a rebellious high-school student who smokes and plays guitar in a western Norwegian village; he has grown up in a Christian environment but decides to leave the state church.

In the 80s, Fosse was primarily a novelist. He also wrote essays and children's books but had no interest in writing plays, despite being encouraged to do so on several occasions. Theater meant nothing to him, if anything he was almost a theater hater. Nevertheless he became a playwright, and his plays today have been translated into more than fifty languages and staged over a thousand times around the world. It all started in 1993, ten years after his debut novel. Fosse wrote a dramatic dialogue for the first time in connection with a competition, and went on to write the play *Someone Is Going to Come*. The main reason was money—Fosse was broke. And writing dialogue ended up going well; the lines flowed out of him strangely easily. Fosse liked the process, it suited him well. He has since called his first experience writing drama "the greatest revelation in my writing life." Starting in the early summer of 1993, Fosse was primarily a playwright.

His work quickly found a place on the important stages in Norway, and within a few years he had established himself as one of the country's leading playwrights. Foreign theaters became interested in his plays as well. The first foreign performance came in 1997, and his major international breakthrough was in 1999, when the acclaimed director Claude Régy staged *Someone Is Going to Come* in France. French newspapers raved about both Fosse and the performance; Fosse was 40 years old at the time and experiencing his great international breakthrough. Along with Régy, the other major director to launch Fosse internationally was Thomas Ostermeier, who in 2000 put on *The Name* with the Schaubühne theater company from Berlin at the Salzburg festival. Fosse wrote more plays at breakneck speed, and soon many were being staged at renowned theaters across Europe.

In a kind of playwriting frenzy, Fosse wrote like a madman and traveled around the world to see how his plays turned out in different places. He had started writing, among other reasons, because it was a way to retreat from the world and be alone, but his international success forced Fosse to be more social—probably more than he would have imagined possible. It was a demanding life, and after some fifteen years as a playwright, Fosse had had enough. He was exhausted. One play had followed the other; he could easily turn out two in a single summer. Rather than writing as a form of retreat, he was now in the limelight, the star attraction at more and more premieres, invited on ever new journeys. Now Fosse no longer wanted to travel, and didn't want to write any more plays either, at least for a while. He wanted to go back to where he had started: fiction.

The prize in Reykjavik reassured Fosse that he was on the right track, that he had not forgotten how to write fiction despite disappearing into the theater. And after rebuking the Prime Minister for claiming his work for Bergen, he could return home to Norway, to the Palace Park in Oslo where he had been granted the lifetime honorary residence The Grotto in 2011. Today, Jon Fosse's closest neighbor is the King of Norway.

Trilogy was the way back to this starting point. The story goes that after Fosse had written the play *I Am the Wind*, he was in such a good flow that he just kept writing. He was worried at the time that his fiction-writing might have dried up in all his playwriting, but he wrote *Wakefulness* almost in one go, quickly and practically without revising. He has called *Wakefulness* the projection of a state, a mood, a sound—it was an old-fashioned narrative. The play *I Am the Wind* is about two men in an imaginary boat where their conversation describes a sailing trip in which one of them takes his own life; the play had its world premiere the same year that *Wakefulness* came out, and Fosse feels there is a connection between the two. *I Am the Wind* is in a way a farewell to life, while *Wakefulness* is the opposite, a book about the life force pushing ahead in defiance of everything. Fosse also has said that despite the book's references to the Christmas story, *Wakefulness* is an immoral text, more pagan than Christian and the least religious work he has written.

Fosse had no plans to write a trilogy—then the years went by and he wondered what had happened to the couple he had written about. How did they turn out? He was a little proud of the fact that they didn't exist until he wrote them into existence, and he set out to write a book about what happened next. And thus the *Trilogy*. He wrote *Olav's Dreams* but didn't publish it until *Weariness* was written as well.

The writing in *Trilogy* is a bit different from most of his earlier fiction but at the same time very recognizable: Fosse sets the action in a mythical past, but as in most of Fosse's texts we find a mixture of past and present, different time periods almost imperceptibly slipping into one another. When Fosse started writing as a boy, he concentrated on the sea, death, and love—so too in *Trilogy*. Luminous love in a large and threatening darkness; fragile and vulnerable people longing for rest and peace. The book is about the basics of life, like being hungry. And *raspeballar*, the western Norwegian potato dumplings that are one of Fosse's personal favorite foods, will never be the same after the scene where Alida is served a full plate of "smoked meat and roasted ham and peas and potatoes and rutabaga and *raspeballar* dumplings." Alida has never tasted anything so good in her life; the grease runs down her chin. *Trilogy* is also, as Fosse's work so often is, about death and suicide: the brutal truth about the short time in which we are an eye in the storm. The movement toward death is found in many of Fosse's works, and he has been criticized for it. But everything is conveyed in Fosse's particular way—rising and falling like waves, rhythmic, singing, lingering, repetitive, and disturbing. It is simple and strangely complex at the same time. Fosse puts it this way: "Writing should be as simple and incomprehensible as life itself."

Fosse is a proponent of Nynorsk, and *Trilogy* uses a far more archaic version of Nynorsk than his previous books. The titles of two of the stories, *Andvake* and *Kveldsvævd*, are words that many young Norwegians today would not understand—not technical terminology but old, beautiful words on their way into obsolescence. *Andvake* means staying sleepless and restless; *Kveldsvævd* means being tired early in the evening, and is also the term for flowers closing up at night as protection against the dark, but without the elevated, intellectual register of the scientific word in English ("nyctinasty").

Hardanger, the area Fosse is from, has a strong tradition of traveling fiddlers. The Hardanger fiddle is one of the most important instruments in Norwegian folk music. Asle is the son of a fiddler and becomes a fiddler himself. And in *Trilogy* it says: "A fiddler's fate is just that, a fate, but he who was without property had to manage as best as he could with the gift God had given him." Fosse sees similarities between writing and playing music and has on several occasions called himself "an itinerant player in life." And much like his other books *Melancholy* and *Septology*, about painters, *Trilogy* is also about art and the nature of art. Fosse uses the verb "float" both for what happens when art is created and for what happens when love is born. Poetic writing "is not like telling, the way a journalist does, or thinking, the way a philosopher does, but it is like acting. It's not music, but it's close," Fosse has said.

Fosse even puts an invented "Jon" in this book. A character named Jon appears at the very end of *Weariness*, a descendant of Asle and Alida who will grow up to be a fiddler and have a book of poems published. "Well, people do all sorts of things, Ales thinks." When asked about this fictional Jon, Fosse has said: "A writer has to be permitted a little wink, a little joke. But who said it was me who shows up in the book? As far as I know, that Jon is publishing a collection of poems, my first book was a novel. Still, it is not entirely unreasonable to read *Trilogy* as my fictional family history."

When Fosse was given the Nordic Council Literature Prize in Reykjavik in 2015, he said that it was fiction he wanted to write in the future. And so he has. At least for a while. We now know that starting then he wrote the most magnificent work in his whole career: *Septology*, a work in seven parts about art, God, alcoholism, friendship, and the passage of time.

CECILIE SEINESS

Wakefulness

I

ASLE AND ALIDA were wandering the streets of Bjørgvin, Asle carried two bundles with everything they owned over his shoulders and in his fist he carried the fiddle case with the fiddle he had inherited from Pa Sigvald, and Alida carried two net bags filled with food, and now they had walked through the streets of Bjørgvin for several hours trying to find lodgings somewhere, but it was impossible to rent anything anywhere, no, they said, sorry but we don't have anything to rent out, no, they said, everything we have to rent out has already been rented, that's what they said and then Asle and Alida had to keep wandering the streets knocking on doors and asking if they could rent a room in a house, but there were no rooms to rent in any of the houses, so where could they go, where could they find shelter from the cold and the darkness now, in late autumn, surely they must be able to rent a room somewhere, a good thing it wasn't raining at least, but soon it might start to rain as well, and they couldn't just walk around like this, and why would no one offer them lodgings, perhaps it was because everyone could see that Alida was soon to give birth, it could happen any day now, the way she looked, or

3

was it because they weren't married and therefore weren't proper husband and wife, couldn't be considered proper people, but surely no one could see that, no, that wasn't possible, or perhaps it was possible after all, because that had to be the reason that no one wanted to rent them a room, and it wasn't because Asle and Alida didn't want to marry that they hadn't had the blessings of the church, how could they have had the time and the means, they were both barely seventeen years old, so obviously they didn't have what was required for a wedding, but as soon as they did, they would get properly married with a priest and a toastmaster and a wedding party and everything that goes with it, but for now that had to wait, for now things had to stay the way they were and they were quite good, really, but why did no one want to offer them a roof over their heads, what was wrong with them, perhaps it would help if they thought of themselves as a properly married man and wife, because if they thought it, it would be more difficult for others to think that they walked around in life as sinners, and now they had knocked on many doors and no one they had asked had wanted to rent them a room and they just couldn't keep going like this, the evening is setting in, it is late autumn, it is dark, it is cold, and soon it might start to rain as well

I'm so tired, Alida says

And they stop and Asle looks at Alida and he doesn't know what he can say to comfort her, because they have already comforted themselves many times talking about the baby, was it a girl or a boy, they talked about that, and Alida thought girls were easier to deal with, and he thought the opposite, it was easier to be with boys, but whether it was a boy or a girl, no matter what they would be happy and grateful for the child they would be parents to before long, they said that and took comfort in thinking about the child which would be born before long. Asle and Alida were wandering the streets of Bjørgvin. And till now they hadn't really worried about it, that no one wanted to offer them lodgings, it would work out in the end, soon there'd be someone who'd have a small room for rent where they could stay for a while, it had to work out, because there were so many houses in Bjørgvin, small houses and large houses, not like in Dylgja, where there were just a few farms and then a few small houses by the sea, she, Alida, was the daughter of Herdis of Brotet, they said, and came from a small homestead in Dylgja, where she grew up with Ma Herdis and her sister Oline, after Pa Aslak disappeared and never came back when Alida was three and her sister Oline five years old, and Alida didn't have a memory of her father, just of his voice, the great sensation that was in his voice, the clear sharp and broad register, but that was all she had left from Pa Aslak, for she couldn't remember anything about his looks, and she couldn't remember anything else either, only his voice when he sang, that was all she had left from Pa Aslak. And he, Asle, grew up in a small Boathouse in Dylgja which was fitted out as a small shelter, he grew up there with Ma Silja and Pa Sigvald, until Pa Sigvald disappeared on the sea one day when the autumn storms came suddenly, he was fishing beyond the islands in the western seas and the boat sank there beyond the islands, beyond Storesteinen. And then Ma Silja and Asle were left in the Boathouse. But not long after Pa Sigvald departed, Ma Silja started to get sick, she grew thinner and thinner, she grew so thin that it was possible to see through her face to her bare bones, her big blue eyes grew bigger and bigger and finally filled most of her face, that's what it looked like to Asle, and her long brown hair grew thinner and more wispy than before, and then, when she didn't get up one morning, Asle found her dead in her bed. Ma Silja was lying there with her big blue eyes open, looking to the side where Pa Sigvald should have been lying. Her long thin brown hair covered most of her face. Ma Silja was lying there dead. This was at least a year ago, when Asle was about sixteen years old. And then all he had in life were himself, the few things in the Boathouse, and the fiddle from Pa Sigvald. Except for Alida, Asle was alone, utterly alone. All he thought of when he saw Ma Silja lying there so grievously dead and gone was Alida. Her long black hair, her black eyes. Everything about her. He had Alida. Now Alida was the only thing left to him. That was all he could think. Asle put his hand on her cold white jaw and stroked her cheek. Now Alida was the only thing he had left. That's what he thought. And then he had the fiddle. He thought that, too. Because his Pa Sigvald had not only been a fisherman, he had also been a great fiddler, and he was the one playing at every wedding in the whole outer Sygna, that's how it was for many years, and if there was to be a dance, one summer night, it was Pa Sigvald who would be playing. And in his time, he had come to Dylgja from the east to play at the wedding of the farmer at Leitet, and that's how he and Asle's mother, Ma Silja, had met, she was a servant girl there and served at the wedding, and Pa Sigvald was playing music. That's how Pa Sigvald and Ma Silja met. And Ma Silja got pregnant. And she gave birth to Asle. And to provide for his family, Pa Sigvald got a job on a fishing boat out in the islands in the sea, the fisherman lived on Storesteinen, and as part of the wages he and Ma Silja could live in a boathouse the fisherman owned there in Dylgja. That's how the fiddler Pa Sigvald became a fisherman as well, living in the Boathouse in Dylgja. That's how it was. That's how it happened. And now both Pa Sigvald and Ma Silja were gone. Gone forever. And now Asle and Alida walked through Bjørgvin's streets, and Asle carried everything they owned in two bundles over his shoulders, and then he had the fiddle case and Pa Sigvald's fiddle with him. It was dark, and it was cold. And now Alida and Asle had knocked on many doors and asked for shelter and their only answer had been that it wasn't possible, there was no room for rent, the room they rented out was already rented, no they didn't rent out rooms, they didn't need to, these were the kind of answers they had been met with, and Asle and Alida walk, they stop, they look at a house, perhaps they have lodgings there, but do they dare knock on that door too, they'll only get a 'no' for an answer again, no matter what, but they couldn't just walk around the streets like this either, so they had to work up the courage to knock and ask if they had a room to rent, but how would Asle or Alida have the determination to once again present their request and once more hear that no, it wasn't possible, it was full enough as it was, things like that, and perhaps they made a mistake when they brought everything they owned with them and sailed into Bjørgvin, but what else should they've done, should they've stayed at Herdis's house in Brotet, even if she didn't want to have them staying there, because there had been no future in that, and if they could've kept living in the Boathouse, they would've stayed there, but one day Asle saw someone, around his own age, come sailing in toward the Boathouse and lower the sails and moor the boat on the foreshore and then he started to walk toward the Boathouse and after a while they heard knocking on the hatch and when Asle had opened and when the man had come in and had finished clearing his throat he said that he owned the Boathouse now that his father had disappeared at sea with Asle's father and now he needed the Boathouse himself, and so naturally Asle and Alida couldn't stay there, and so they had to pack their things and find somewhere else to live, that's all there is to it, he said, and then he walked over to the bed next to Alida who sat there with her big stomach and she stood up and walked over to Asle and then the man lay down on the bed and stretched out and he said that he was tired and now he wanted to have a rest, he said, and Asle looked at Alida and then they walked over to the hatch and lifted it up. And then they walked down the steps and out and stood in front of the Boathouse. Alida with her big stomach and Asle.

Now we have nowhere to live, Alida said

and Asle didn't answer

But it's his boathouse, so there's nothing we can do about it, I suppose, Asle said

We don't have anywhere to stay, Alida said

It's late autumn, it's dark and cold, and we have to have somewhere to live, she said

and then they stood there in silence

And I'm going to give birth soon, I could give birth any day now, she says

Yes, Asle says

And we have nowhere to stay, she says

and then she sits down on the bench at the wall of the boathouse, the one his Pa Sigvald had built

I should have killed him, Asle says

Don't says things like that, Alida says

and then Asle goes and sits down next to Alida there on the bench

I'll murder him, Asle says

No, no, Alida says

That's just how it is, there are some people who own things and some people who don't, she says

And those who own decide over those who don't, she says

I suppose that's how it is, Asle says

And that's how it must be, Alida says

I suppose it must, Asle says

and Alida and Asle remain sitting there on the bench without saying anything and after a while the man who owns the Boathouse comes out and he says they'll have to pack what belongs to them, because now he lives in the Boathouse, he says, and he doesn't want them there, at least not Asle, he says, but Alida, however, she can stay, the state she's in, he says, he'll be back in a couple of hours, and then they, at least Asle, must be out and gone, he says, and then he goes down to his boat and while he's loosening the mooring he says that he is dropping by the shopkeeper for a moment and when he comes back the Boathouse must be empty and ready, he's going to sleep there tonight, and yes perhaps Alida too, if she wants to, he says, and he pushes off and he hoists the sails and then his boat glides northward along the coast.

I can pack, Asle says

I can help you, Alida says

No, you go home to Brotet, go home to Ma Herdis, Asle says

Perhaps we can sleep there tonight, he says

Perhaps, Alida says

and she stands up and Asle watches her walk along the foreshore, her quite short legs, her round hips, her long black thick hair billowing down her back, and Asle sits there and watches Alida and she turns and looks at him and then she lifts her arm and waves and then she begins to walk up toward Brotet and then Asle walks into the Boathouse and he packs everything there in two bundles and then he walks along the foreshore with two bundles over his shoulders and the fiddle box in his hand and out on the sea he can see the man who owns the Boathouse come sailing in his boat and Asle walks up toward Brotet and he is carrying everything he owns in two bundles over his shoulders, apart from the fiddle and the fiddle box, which he holds in one hand and after a while he sees Alida come walking toward him and she says they cannot stay with Ma Herdis, because Herdis had never liked her, her own daughter, not very much, she had always liked her sister Oline much better, and she had never understood why it was like that, so she didn't want to go there, not now, when her stomach has grown so big and everything, she says, and Asle says that it's getting late, and soon it'll be dark, and now in late autumn it's cold at night, and perhaps it'll start raining too, so they'll just have to give in and ask if they can stay for a while at Herdis's house in Brotet, he says, and Alida says that if that's what they have to do then he has to ask, she won't do it, she'd rather sleep wherever it may be, she says, and Asle says that if he must ask he will ask and when they are standing in the hallway Asle says as it is true that the man who owns the Boathouse now wants to live there himself, so they have nowhere to live, but could

they possibly stay here at Herdis's house for a while, Asle
says, and Herdis says that oh well if that's how it is yes then
all she can do is let them stay then, but only for a while,
she says, and then she says they'll have to come up then
and then Herdis walks toward the stairs and then Asle and
Alida walk after her and then Herdis goes up into the loft
and then she says they can stay here for a while but not for
too long, and then she turns and goes downstairs and Asle
puts down the bundles with everything they own on the
floor and he puts the fiddle case in the corner and Alida
says that her Ma Herdis has never liked her, never, no she
never had, and she has never quite understood why she
didn't like her and Herdis probably didn't like Asle much
either, she disliked him, simple as that, if truth be told,
that's the way it was and when Alida was pregnant and
she and Asle weren't married, yes Herdis probably couldn't
live with the shame in her house, that's probably what she
thought, her mother, even if she didn't say it, Alida said,
so here, they could only stay here tonight, just one single
night, Alida said, and Asle said that then, if that was how
it was, yes he didn't know any other solution than that they
had to get into Bjørgvin tomorrow already, because they
had to be able to find somewhere to stay there, he'd been
there once, he said, in Bjørgvin, he said, with Pa Sigvald,
he'd been there, and he remembered so well how it was,
the streets, the houses, all the people, the sounds and the
smells, all the shops, all the things in the shops, he remembered everything so clearly, he said, and when Alida asked
how they would get to Bjørgvin, Asle said that they had
to find a boat and sail there

    Find a boat, Alida said

    Yes, Asle said

What boat, Alida said

There's a boat moored in front of the Boathouse, Asle said

But that boat, Alida said

and then she saw Asle standing up and walking out and Alida lay down on the bed up there in the loft and then she stretched out and she closed her eyes and she is so tired and so tired and she sees Pa Sigvald sitting there with his fiddle and he picks up a bottle and takes a large swig and then she sees Asle standing there, his black eyes, his black hair, and she got a shock, for there he stood, there stood her boy, and then she sees Pa Sigvald waving to Asle and he goes to his father and she sees Asle sitting there and he lays the fiddle under his chin and then he begins to play and at the same time she is sinking and she is lifted up and she rises and rises and in his playing she hears Pa Aslak singing and she hears her own life and her own future and she knows what she knows and then she is present there in her own future and everything is open and everything is difficult but the song, that is there and this must be the song they call love and then she is only present in the playing and she doesn't want to exist any other place and then her Ma Herdis comes and asks what she's doing, shouldn't she have gone to bring water to the cows a long time ago, shouldn't she have shovelled the snow, what did she think, did she think Ma Herdis should do everything, look after the house, take care of the animals, cook, wasn't it difficult enough for them to do what had to be done if she wasn't always, constantly, shirking her duties, oh no, that didn't work, she had to pull herself together, she should take a good look at her sister Oline, how she was always helping and doing the best she could, how could two sisters be so different, both

in looks and otherwise, how could that happen, one looking like her father, the other like her mother, that's how
it was, there's no getting away from that, and that's how
it always would be, Ma Herdis said, and why should she
help with anything anyway when Ma Herdis was always
criticizing her and yelling at her, she was the evil one and
her sister Oline the good one, she was the black one and
her sister Oline the white one, and Alida stretches out on
the bed and what's going to happen now, where are they
going to stay, she's going to give birth any time now, the
Boathouse wasn't a grand place, but it was somewhere to
live and now they weren't even allowed to be there and
now they had nowhere to stay, and money, no they had
almost none of that, she had a few bills, and Asle had a few
as well, but it wasn't much, as good as nothing, but they
would be able to manage, she was sure of that, they would
manage, but if only Asle would come back soon, because
that thing about the boat, no she must not think about
that, be that as it may, and Alida could hear Ma Herdis
saying that now she's just as dark and ugly as her father,
and just as lazy, always shirking her duties, Ma Herdis says,
how's she going to cope, at least it's a good thing that it's
her sister Oline who'll take over the farm, because Alida
would've been useless, that would've been a mess, she hears
her mother saying and then she hears her sister Oline say
that it's a good thing it's her who'll take over the farm, the
fine farm they have here in Brotet, her sister Oline says,
and Alida hears her mother saying what'll happen with
Alida, no she has no idea and Alida says not to worry, she
doesn't care anyway, and then Alida walks out and she goes
over to the Knoll where she and Asle have made it their
habit to meet and when she now approaches she can see

Asle sitting there and he looks pale and worn and she can
see that his black eyes are wet and she knows something
has happened and then Asle looks at her and he says that
Ma Silja is dead and now Alida is the only one he has left
and he lies down on his back and Alida goes and lies down
beside him and he puts his arms around her and he holds
her close and then he says that he found his mother dead
this morning, she was lying there in bed and her big blue
eyes filled her whole face, he says, and he holds Alida close
and then they disappear into each other and only the soft
sound of the wind in the trees can be heard and they are
gone and they are shameful and they kill and they talk and
no longer think and then they lie there on the Knoll and
they are shameful and they sit up and then they sit there
on the Knoll and look out across the sea

Imagine doing something like that the day Ma Silja
dies, Asle says

Yes, Alida says

and Asle and Alida stand up and then they stand there
and set their clothes straight and then they stand there and
look at the islands in the sea to the west, at Storesteinen

You're thinking about Pa Sigvald, Alida says

Yes, Asle says

and he lifts his hand up in the air and stands there and
holds it against the wind

But you have me, Alida says

And you have me, Asle says

and then Asle begins to wave his hand back and forth,
he waves

You're waving to your parents, Alida says

Yes, Asle says

You can feel them too, he says

Yes that they're here, he says

Both of them are here now, he says

and then Asle lowers his hand and he moves it toward Alida and he strokes her cheek and then he takes her hand in his and then they stand there like that

But imagine, Alida says

Yes, Asle says

Imagine if, Alida says

and she puts her other hand on her stomach

Yes imagine that, Asle says

and then they smile at each other and then they begin to walk hand in hand down Brotet and then Alida can see that Asle is standing on the floor there in the loft and his hair is wet and there is pain in his face and he looks tired and worn

Where have you been, Alida says

No, nowhere, Asle says

But you're wet and cold, she says

and then she says that Asle must come and lie down and he just stands there

But don't just stand there, she says

and he just stands there, rigid

What is it, she says

and he says they'll have to go, the boat's ready

But don't you want to get some sleep, Alida says

We should go, he says

Just a little, you must get some rest, she says

Not much, just a little, she says

You're tired, Asle says

Yes, Alida says

You slept, he says

I think so, she says

and he keeps standing there on the floor, there under
the slanted ceiling

But come then, she says

and she stretches her arms out to him

We must go soon, he says

But where, she says

To Bjørgvin, he says

But how, she says

We're sailing, he says

Then we must have a boat, she says

I've arranged a boat, Asle says

Let's have a little rest first, she says

Just a little one then, he says

Then our clothes can dry a little too, he says

and Asle undresses and spreads his clothes out on the
floor and Alida lifts the woollen blanket and Asle comes
into bed with her and he lies close to her and she feels how
cold and wet he is and she asks if everything went well
and he says that yes, yes it did, yes and he asks if she has
slept and she says she thinks she has and he says they can
have a little rest now and then they must bring some food,
as much as they possibly can, and perhaps some money
as well, if they can find some somewhere, and then they
must go down to the boat and sail away before daylight
and morning and she says that yes, they'll have to do what
he thinks is best, she says, and then they lie there and she
sees Asle sitting there with his fiddle and she stands and
listens and she hears the song from her own past, and she
hears the song from her own future, and she hears Aslak
singing, and she knows that everything is destined and
that this is how it should be and she puts her hand over
her stomach and the child is kicking again and then she

hears Asle saying that no, they ought to leave now while it's dark, that's best, he says, and he's so tired, he says, that if he falls asleep now, he could sleep very soundly for a long time, but he can't do that, they must get into the boat, Asle says, and he sits up in bed

Can't we lie here just a bit longer, Alida says

You lie there for a bit longer, Asle says

and he stands up on the floor and Alida asks if she should put out the lamp and he says no she doesn't need to and he starts to dress and Alida asks if his clothes are dry, no, he says, they're not dry, but they're not so wet either, he says, and he puts his clothes on and Alida sits up in bed

Now we're going to Bjørgvin, he says

We're going to live in Bjørgvin, Alida says

Yes, yes we are, Asle says

and Alida steps out onto the floor and she puts out the light and only now can she see how wild and haunted Asle looks and she starts to put her clothes on.

But where will we live, she says

We'll have to find a house somewhere, he says

We should be able to, he says

There are so many houses in Bjørgvin, there's so much of everything there, so that'll work out, he says

If there's no room for us in any of all those houses in Bjørgvin, I don't know what then, Asle says

and he picks up both bundles and lifts them up on his shoulders and he takes the fiddle case in his hand and Alida takes the light and then she opens the door and she goes out ahead of him and then she walks slowly and quietly down the stairs and he walks quietly down the stairs after her

I'll get some food, Alida says

Good, Asle says

I'll wait out in the yard, he says

and Asle walks into the hallway and Alida walks into the larder and she finds two net bags and she puts cured meats and flatbread and butter in the bags and then she walks into the hallway and she opens the door and she sees Asle standing there in the yard and she holds the bags out to him and he comes and takes them

But what'll your mother say, he says

She can say whatever she likes, Alida says

Yes but, he says

and Alida walks into the hallway again and into the kitchen and she knows where her mother hides her money, there on the top of the cupboard, in a chest, and Alida finds a stool and she puts it against the cupboard and then she climbs onto the stool and she opens the cupboard and there, at the back, she gets hold of the chest and she jiggles it loose and she opens the chest and she takes the bills that are there and she pushes the chest back in the cupboard and she closes the door to the cupboard and she stands there with the bills in her hand and then the door to the living room opens and she sees her mother's face in the light she holds up in front of her

What are you doing, Ma Herdis says

and Alida stands there and then she climbs down from the stool

What've you got in your hand, her mother says

No you, she says

No what's become of you, she says

So you've come this far now, she says, stealing

I'll get you, she says

You're stealing from your own mother, she says

How can it be possible, she says
You're just like your father, you are, she says
Rabble like him, she says
And a slut you are too, she says
Look at you, she says
Give me the money, she says
Give me the money now, she says
You whore, Ma Herdis says
and then she grabs Alida's hand
Let me go, Alida says
Let go, Ma Herdis says
Let go, you whore, she says
No way I'll let go, Alida says
Stealing from your own mother, Ma Herdis says
and Alida hits out at Ma Herdis with her free hand
You're hitting your own mother, Ma Herdis says
No you're worse than your father, she says
I won't let anyone hit me, she says
and Herdis grabs Alida's hair and pulls and Alida
screams and then she grabs Ma Herdis's hair and pulls and
then Asle stands there and he takes Herdis's hair and loos-
ens the grip and then he stands there and holds her tight
Go outside, Asle says
I'm going, Alida says
Yes go, he says
Take the money and go out into the yard and wait
there, Asle says
and Alida holds on to the money and walks into the
yard and she stands there next to the bundles and the net
bags and it is cold and she can see the stars and the moon
is shining and she cannot hear anything and then she sees
Asle coming out of the house and he walks over to her

and she hands him the bills and he takes them and folds them and then he puts them into a pocket and then Alida takes a bag in each hand and Asle lifts the bundles with everything they own over his shoulders and he takes the fiddle case in his hand and then he says that they should be off and then they start walking down Brotet and none of them says anything and it's a clear night with twinkling stars and a shining moon and they walk down Brotet and down there is the Boathouse and there is the boat, moored

Can we just take the boat, Alida says

Yes we can, Asle says

But, Alida says

We can safely take the boat, Asle says

We can take the boat and we can sail to Bjørgvin, he says

You don't need to be afraid, he says

and Alida and Asle walk down to the boat and he pulls it ashore and puts the bundles and the net bags and the fiddle case in the boat, and Alida steps in, and then Asle unties the mooring and then he rows the boat a way out on the water and he says that the weather's good, the moon's shining, the stars are twinkling, it's cold and clear, and there's a good wind for a calm sail southward, he says, so now they can sail to Bjørgvin and that should be no problem, he says, and Alida doesn't want to ask if he knows the way and Asle says he remembers the time he and his Pa Sigvald sailed to Bjørgvin, he knows just about where to sail, he says, and Alida sits there on the thwart and she sees Asle pulling in the oars and hoisting the sails and then she sees him sitting down there by the tiller and then the boat glides out and away from Dylgja and Alida turns and she sees the house there in Brotet, that's how light it is this late-autumn night, and the house there looks decadent,

and she sees the Knoll where she and Asle used to meet,
and where she got pregnant, where the child she is soon to
give birth to was made, that is her place, that is where she
belongs and Alida sees the Boathouse where she and Asle
lived for a few months and then the boat glides around
the headland and then she sees mountains and islets and
reefs and the boat glides slowly forward

Why don't you lie down and sleep, Asle says

Can I do that, Alida says

Of course, Asle says

Wrap yourself up in the woollen blanket, and then lie
down in the front of the boat, he says

and Alida opens one of the bundles and takes out the
four blankets they have and she makes a bed for herself
there in the front of the boat and she wraps herself up in a
blanket and then she lies there listening to the sea sloshing
against the boat and she falls into the light swaying and she
feels nice and warm as she lies there, in this cold night, and
she looks up at the clear stars and the round shining moon

Now life begins, she says

Now we're sailing into life, he says

I don't think I can sleep, she says

But you can lie there and rest, he says

It's good to lie here, she says

It's good you feel good, he says

Yes things are good, she says

and then she hears the sea coming, and the sea going,
and the moon is shining and the night is like a strange day
and the boat is drifting and drifting forward, southward,
along the foreshore

Aren't you tired, she says

No, I'm wide awake, he says

And then she sees Ma Herdis in front of her as she stands there calling her a whore and then she sees her mother one Christmas Eve coming into the living room with the mutton ribs, happy and beautiful and good without any of the pain she often suffered from, and she just left, she didn't even say goodbye to her Ma Herdis, and not to her sister Oline either, she just took what food she could find and put it in the two net bags and then she took what money there was in the house and then she just left and she will doubtlessly never again, never again see Ma Herdis, she knows that, and she has seen the house there in Brotet for the last time, she's certain of that, and she'll never again see Dylgja, if only she hadn't just left, then she could have gone to her mother and said that she would never trouble her again, now or later in life, she was leaving now, they were finished with each other now, she would have said, they would never trouble each other again and she would never see her again just as she never saw Pa Aslak again after he disappeared and was gone, she'd leave now and never come back and when Ma Herdis asked where they would go, Alida would say that she shouldn't worry about that and Ma Herdis would say that she would in any case give her a little food for the journey and then Ma Herdis would take out the chest with the bills and give her a few and then she'd have said that she wouldn't send her daughter away from her and into the big world totally penniless and she would never see her mother again and Alida opens her eyes and she sees that the stars are now gone and there's no more night and she sits up and she sees Asle sitting there at the helm

Are you awake, he says

That's good, he says

And good morning to you, he says

Good morning to you too, she says

It's good you're awake because we'll soon be sailing into
Vågen, in Bjørgvin, he says

and Alida stands up and she sits down on the thwart
and she looks southward

We'll be there soon, Asle says

Over there, look, he says

We'll follow this fjord and then go around a headland
and then we'll be in Byfjorden, he says

And then, when we've arrived in Byfjorden, then we'll
just sail straight into Vågen, he says

and Alida sees only hills on both sides of the fjord, not
a single house in sight and they are sailing toward Bjørgvin
and the wind is subsiding, and they are just floating, they
eat cured meat and flatbread and drink water with it, they
get a little wind and then they get a good wind and then
they sail until they drift into Vågen in the afternoon and
they moored there at the Wharf and then Asle went ashore
and asked if someone wanted to buy a boat from him, there
wasn't a great deal of interest, but when he kept cutting the
price he managed to sell the boat for a bit of money. And
then they had that money as well. And then Asle and Alida
stood there on the Wharf with the two bundles, and with
the two bags, and with the fiddle case and his Pa Sigvald's
fiddle and a few bills, they had those as well. And then they
started to walk and where they walked was less important,
Asle said, they should just have a walk and look around,
and even if he had been in Bjørgvin before, he couldn't
say he knew it all that well, he said, but big, yes, the city
of Bjørgvin was big, it was one of the biggest, perhaps
the very biggest, city in Norway, he said, and Alida said

that she, yes she had never before been further away than
Torsvik, and that was a big thing for her, so now, here,
here in this big city of Bjørgvin with houses and people
everywhere, no she couldn't find her way around here, it
would take years for her to feel at home here, Alida said,
but it was exciting to be here, yes it was, so much to see,
so much happening all the time, she said, and Asle and
Alida walked along the Wharf with all the tower houses
on the upper side, and then all the boats moored below
the houses, boats of all kinds, four-oared boats and boats
with a high upright stem and whatever kind of boats you
could think of

And over there is the Market Place, Asle said

The Market Place, Alida said

Haven't you heard about the Market Place in Bjørgvin,
he said

Yes perhaps I have, when I think about it, Alida said

That's where people from the countryside like me and
you sell their goods, Asle said

Yes, Alida said

They come in with their boats and with fish and meat
and vegetables and whatever they have to sell, and then
they sell it there, at the Market Place

But no one from Dylgja comes there, do they, Alida says

I'd think that sometimes they do, Asle says

And he points, and there, beyond all the moored boats,
there is the Market Place, there, you can see all the people
and all the stalls, that's where it is, he says, and Alida says
that they don't have to go there, do they, why don't they
go over to the other side of the street, there are less people
there and it's easier to make their way there, she says, and
then they cross the street and on the hill behind them

they see that there are many houses, so they suppose they should go among all the houses and ask for lodgings, Asle says, there are so many houses, surely they'll be able to rent something there, he says

And then, Asle says

Yes, Alida says

And then I must go out again and find work, because we have to have an income, he says

You want to ask for work, Alida says

Yes, Asle says

Where, Alida says

I suppose I'll have to go down to the Market Place, or out on the Wharf and ask there, Asle says

And perhaps I can find some tavern I can play in, he says

and Alida doesn't say anything and they walk down the street between the houses and Alida says that they can't just knock on the door of the first and best house and Asle says why not and they stop and Asle knocks on the door and an old woman comes out and she looks at them and she says yes and Asle asks if she has a room for rent in her house and the old woman repeats room for rent and then she says that they'll have to ask for a room for rent where they come from and not here in Bjørgvin, they don't need more people here, she says, and then she closes the door and they can hear her say room for rent room for rent as she limps back into her house room for rent room for rent and they look at each other and grin and then they walk over to the other side of the street and knock on the house there and after a little while a girl comes out and she looks at them, a little bewildered, and when Asle asks if they have a room for rent in their house she grins and says they'll probably have a room for him but it's another matter with her, if she'd come a few months earlier they would've found a room for her too, but now, the way she was now, it's another matter, the Girl says, and then she stands there and leans against the door frame and she looks at Asle

Are you coming in or, the Girl says

I can't be standing here, she says

Answer me, then, she says

and then Alida looks at Asle and she takes his sleeve

Come let's go, Alida says

Yes, Asle says

Yes why don't you go, the Girl says

Come, Alida says

And she pulls Asle gently and then the Girl chortles and goes inside and closes the door and they can hear her say no it's not possible, such a fine boy and such a little hussy, she says, and then someone answers it's always like that, that's usually the case, someone says, and someone else says, always, it's always like that and then Alida and Asle keep walking down the street and they walk for quite a while along a group of houses

She was awful, Alida says

Yes, Asle says

and they keep walking and they stop in front of the door of yet another house, they knock and no matter who opens, no one has anything to rent out, they haven't got space, they don't rent out rooms, the wife isn't at home, it's one thing or another, but one thing is the same, they don't have anything to rent out and then Asle and Alida keep walking by all the houses, most of them are small houses, very close together, and a narrow street sneaks between the houses, and sometimes there's a slightly broader street between the houses, and where they are and where they walk, no, neither Asle nor Alida know that, and that it would be so difficult to find a roof over their heads in Bjørgvin, to find shelter from the cold and the dark, no they had never imagined that, because Asle and Alida had been wandering the streets of Bjørgvin for the whole after-noon and evening, knocking on one door after another, they asked one person after another and they got answers, many different answers, but mostly they were told that no, there was no room for rent, the room was already rented, that's what they were told and now Alida and Asle had been wandering the streets of Bjørgvin for a long time and now they stop and they stand very still and Asle looks at Alida, her long black thick wavy hair, her sad black eyes

I'm so tired, Alida says

And Asle sees that his dear, dear girl looks so tired and it can't be good for a pregnant woman who is soon to give birth to be as tired as Alida is now perhaps, no it cannot be good

Can we sit down for a while soon, Alida says

Yes I suppose we can, Asle says

and they keep trudging along and then it starts to rain and they just keep trudging along, walking like this in the rain and getting wet, and the chill is creeping into their bodies, it's dark now, it's cold now, for it's late autumn and they have nowhere to seek shelter from the rain and the cold and the dark and if only they had somewhere to sit down, a warm room, yes if they only had that

I'm tired, yes, Alida says

And now it's raining too, she says

We have to at least find a place where we can be under a roof, Asle says

No we cannot walk around in the rain getting wet, he says

No, Alida says

and she picks up her bags and then she trudges along in the rain

Are you cold, Asle says

Yes, yes I'm wet and cold, Alida says

and they stop, they stand there in the rain, in the street, and then they go and stand up against a wall, under the eave, and they stand there, holding themselves up against the wall

What are we going to do, Alida says

We have to find shelter for the night, she says

Yes, Asle says

We must have knocked on twenty doors at least to ask for a room, Alida says

More than that, Asle says

And no one wants us in their house, she says

No, he says

It's too cold to sleep outside, and we're so wet, she says

Yes, he says

and they stand there for a long time without saying anything and it's raining and it's cold and it's dark and now there is no one else out in the streets, earlier today there were so many people out in the streets, all sorts of people, young, old, but now it seems they're indoors in their houses, in the light and the warmth, because now the rain is coming down and down from the sky forming puddles at their feet and Alida looks at her bags, and she squats down and her chin falls on her chest and her eyelids fall down over her eyes and then Alida sits there and sleeps and Asle is so tired as well, so tired, it's such a long time since

they were lying there in Herdis's house in Brotet unable to
sleep and then got up and took the boat and began sailing southward to Bjørgvin, the long crossing to Bjørgvin,
but that went well, they had a good wind for most of the
night, the wind only calmed late morning and they were
gliding there and now Asle is so tired he could sleep where
he is standing, but he mustn't, no he mustn't sleep now,
but he closes his eyes and he sees that the fjord is calm and
glitteringly blue, and the sea out there is glitteringly blue,
and the boat is bobbing lightly in the cove, and the hills
around the Boathouse are green, and he sits on the bench
and he holds his fiddle in his hand and he puts his fiddle
against his shoulder and he plays and there, over there in
Brotet, there Alida comes running and it's as if his playing and her movements blend with the light and green
day and a happiness so big makes his playing become one
with everything that grows and breathes and he feels that
his love for Alida flows and flows in him and it flows over
into his playing and it flows into everything that grows
and breathes and Alida comes over to him and she sits
down on the bench next to him and he just keeps playing
and Alida puts a hand on his thigh and he plays and plays
and his playing is as high as the sky and as spacious as the
sky, because they met each other yesterday, Alida and Asle,
and they agreed that she should come down to him, but
they had still barely spoken, yesterday was the first time
they had spoken, but they had seen each other and felt
drawn to each other since they had become grown-ups
and reached the age where boys notice girls and girls notice
boys, already the first time they saw each other, they saw
each other deeply, they both knew that, without anything
being said, and last night they spoke together and got to

know each other for the first time, for last night Asle was
with Pa Sigvald when he played at the wedding at Leitet
farm, where Pa Sigvald also played that evening and night
he met Ma Silja, at that time it was the farmer at Leitet
who got married, and last night it was his daughter, and
when Asle heard that Pa Sigvald was going to play at the
wedding, he asked if he could come

Yes I suppose you could, Pa Sigvald said

I suppose I can only say yes, he said

There's no way around it, you'll become a fiddler too,
he said

and Pa Sigvald said if that's what it was like, that he was
a fiddler and should be a fiddler, then that's how it was,
he was a good player already, as far as playing goes he was
already an accomplished fiddler, and if you were a fiddler,
then you were a fiddler, there was little and nothing to do
about that, he would become a fiddler, his son as well, and
that was not a surprise, because both his father, old Asle,
and his grandfather, old Pa Sigvald, had been fiddlers, to be
a fiddler was a family fate, even if being a fiddler was reck-
oned to be bad luck, yes that it was, Pa Sigvald said, but if
you were a fiddler yes then you were a fiddler, if that's how
it was, yes, there was nothing to do about that, not much,
yes, in his opinion, said Pa Sigvald, and if he was asked
where it came from, he answered that it probably came
from grief, grieving over something, or just grief, and in
the music the grief could lighten and become soaring and
the soaring could become happiness and joy, so therefore
music was needed, therefore he had to play, and some people had something left of this grief and that's why there
were many who enjoyed listening to the playing, that's
how it was, because the music lifted their life and gave it

height, whether they were holding a wake or celebrating
a wedding or people were just meeting to dance and cel-
ebrate, but why they were the only ones who were given
the fate of the fiddler, yes he couldn't say why, of course
not, and he had never had much knowledge or wisdom,
but he'd been a good fiddler since he was just a boy, since
he was Asle's age, just like Asle was a good fiddler now
too, they were alike in so many things he and Asle, Pa
Sigvald said, and just as he had followed his father when
he was Asle's age and his granddad was playing in a wedding, now Asle was going to follow his father and get his
training, and later in the summer he would come with his
father when he played at an ordinary dance and he would
come with his father when he played at a wake, the way he
himself had come with his father, to weddings, wakes, and
dances, but whether he liked it, whether he liked that his
son should also become a fiddler, no that was something
else altogether, and no one would ask about that anyway,
a fiddler's fate is just that, a fate, but he who was without
property had to manage as best as he could with the gift
God had given him, that's how it was, that was life

And tonight you'll try to be a fiddler, Pa Sigvald said

and he said that they could walk together to the wedding and when he had played for a while, then Asle could
take over the fiddle and play a tune or two, he said

I'll play till the dance has gotten properly started, and
then you take over the fiddle, he said

and then both Pa Sigvald and Asle dressed up in their
best clothes and Ma Silja gave them some nice food, and
she said they had to behave and not drink too much or
be tempted into foolishness, she said, and then Pa Sigvald
walked with the fiddle case in one hand and next to him

walked Asle and when they had walked for a while and were approaching Leitet his father sat down and took out the fiddle, he tuned it and played a few chords, and then he took a bottle from the case and took a deep swig and then he played a little more, carefully, as if he was feeling his way, and then Pa Sigvald held out the bottle to Asle and told him to take a swig and Asle did and then he held out the fiddle to Asle and told him to warm up on the fiddle and also to warm himself up, the playing was always best if it happened like that, that you played yourself slowly up to it, from almost nothing and up, from nothing and then up to something enormous, he said, and then Asle sat there and tried to play himself up from almost nothing, he began to play almost right down at the bottom, and then slowly and as low as he only could, he played himself up

Yes that's right, Pa Sigvald said

You're already a master fiddler, he said

You're playing yourself up as if you've never done anything else, he said

and then Pa Sigvald took another swig from the bottle and Asle handed him the fiddle and Pa Sigvald handed the bottle to Asle and he took another swig and then they sat there without saying anything.

The fate of the fiddler is fatal, Pa Sigvald then said

Always away, always going away, he said

Yes, Asle said

Yes, going away from your dear ones, and from yourself, Pa Sigvald said

Always giving yourself to others, he said

Always, he said

Never being quite wholly your own, he said

Always trying to make others whole

and then Pa Sigvald said that everything to him was in his love for Ma and Asle, and he didn't want to travel around and play, but what else could he do, what did he own, nothing, not a single thing, the only thing was the fiddle and himself and then this damned fiddler's fate, Pa Sigvald said, and then he stood up and said that they'd better go over to Leitet farm and do what they were meant to do and which they were paid for and then he said that Asle could just stay there in the yard, doing what he wanted to do, and later, tonight, when the dance had gotten properly going, he could come in and stand where he could see him and then he'd wave Asle over and take a break and then Asle could take over the fiddle

And then you play a tune or two, Pa Sigvald said

And then you too will have become a fiddler, he said

That's how your grandad, the one you're named after, started as a fiddler, he says

And now you'll start like that as well, he says

And that's how I started in my time, he says

and Asle hears something hazy in Pa Sigvald's voice and he looks at him and he sees that he's standing there and there are tears in his eyes and then Asle sees the tears starting to run down his father's cheeks and his cheeks tighten and then he puts the back of his hand up to his eyes and he wipes away the tears

Off we go, Pa Sigvald said

and then Asle watched Pa Sigvald's back as he was walking along and he saw that the long hair, held together with a piece of twine at the back of the neck, the hair that had been black, as black as Asle's hair, now had a lot of gray in it, and it had become quite thin too and Pa Sigvald is walking a little heavily, and he's not so young anymore,

but not so old either, and Asle hears a voice saying that
they can't stay here and he opens his eyes and he sees a tall
black hat there in front of him and he sees a bearded face
and a man is standing there with a long stick in one hand
and in the other he holds a lantern and he holds the lantern up in front of Asle's face and then he looks straight
into Asle's face

You can't stand here and sleep, the Man says

You two can't sleep here, the Man repeats and Asle sees
that the Man is wearing a long black coat

You have to leave, the Man says

Yes, Asle says

But we don't know where to go, he says

You don't have anywhere to stay, the Man says

No, Asle says

Then I should take you with me and put you in the
lockup, the Man says

Have we done something wrong, Asle says

Not yet, the Man says

and then he chortles a little and then he lowers the
lantern

It's not summer now, the Man says

It's late autumn, cold and chilly, he says

But where can we find somewhere to stay, Asle says

You're really asking me, the Man says

Yes, Asle says

There are many taverns and inns here in Bjørgvin, the
Man says

There are several here in Inste Street, he says

Taverns and inns, Asle says

Yes, the Man says

And we can get a room there, Asle says

Oh yes, the Man says

But where, Asle says

There's one over there, just a bit further down the street, there on the other side, the Man says

and he looks and points

It says Inn on the wall, he says

But of course you'll have to pay for yourselves, he says

Go there, why don't you, he says

and then the Man goes and Asle sees Alida sitting there squatting and sleeping with her chin down on her chest, and she can't stay here, of course not, in this cold, this dark, this rain, now in late autumn, but for just a little while, they could rest for just a little while, that'll do them good and Asle is so tired, he feels so tired that he could lie right down and fall asleep and lie there and sleep for a week and then he too squats and he puts his hand on Alida's hair and her hair is wet and he strokes her hair and he runs his fingers through her hair and he closes his eyes and he feels so heavy and so tired and then he sees Pa Sigvald sitting there in the living room at Leitet, playing, and his long hair, black and gray, is held together with a piece of rope at the back of the neck and Pa Sigvald lifts the bow and the tune wafts in the air and then he stands up and takes a swig from the bottle and he takes a swig from the tankard and then Pa Sigvald looks around and he sees Asle and he waves Asle over and then he hands Asle the fiddle

Now it's your turn, Asle, Pa Sigvald says

yes, that's the way it is, yes, he says

And you'll get a little swig as well, he says

and he hands Asle the bottle and he takes a deep swig and then he takes another swig and he hands the bottle to Pa Sigvald, and he hands the mug to Asle

You'll have to have a sip of beer too, he says

A fiddler has to have something to fortify himself with, Pa Sigvald says

and Asle takes a gulp of beer and gives the mug back to Pa Sigvald and then he sits down on the stool and he puts the fiddle in his lap and plucks the strings and tunes the fiddle and then he places the fiddle on his shoulder and he begins to play and it doesn't sound too bad and he keeps playing and people begin to dance and he keeps playing and pushes on, he doesn't want to give up, he just wants to keep going, he wants to force out the pounding grief, he wants the grief to become light, to lighten and lift up, to take flight and flow upward without weight, he'll make that happen and he plays and plays and then he finds the place where the music lifts and then it soars yes, yes, yes it soars yes and then he doesn't have to keep playing, then the music is soaring above all by itself and it's playing its own world and everyone who can hear, they can hear it and Asle looks up and he sees her standing there, she stands there, he sees Alida standing there, she stands there with her long black wavy hair and her large sad black eyes. And she hears it. She hears the soaring and she is in the soaring. She stands still and she soars. And then they soar together, now they soar together, she and he. Alida and Asle. And he sees Pa Sigvald's face and he smiles, there is happiness to see in his smile and Pa Sigvald lifts the bottle to his mouth and takes a deep swig. And Asle lets the playing play. And Alida is with him. He can see in her eyes that Alida is with him. And Asle lets the soaring soar. And as it soars lightly along he lifts the bow and lets the soaring ascend into the emptiness. And Asle stands up and he hands the fiddle to Pa Sigvald and he puts his arms around Asle's shoulders

and holds him close against him. And Pa Sigvald stands
with the fiddle in his hand and holds Asle close. And then
Pa Sigvald tosses his head, puts the fiddle to his shoulder
and he taps the beat and then he begins to play. And Asle
walks toward Alida, where she stands with her long black
wavy hair and her large sad black eyes. And Alida walks
toward him, and then Asle puts his hand on her shoulder
and they walk out and none of them says anything before
they are out in the yard and there they stop and Asle takes
his hand away

So you're Asle, Alida says

And you're Alida, Asle says

And then they stand there without saying anything

We've never talked before, Asle says

No, Alida says

And then they stand there and they say nothing

But I've seen you before, Alida says

And I've seen you, Asle says

and then they stand there and don't say anything

You played so well, Alida says

Thank you, Asle says

I'm a servant girl here at Leitet, Alida says

And today I've been serving at the wedding, but now
that the dance has started I don't have to work, she says

My ma was a servant girl here too, Asle says

Shall we go for a walk, he says

Why not, Alida says

And over there, yes there's the Knoll, where you can see
right out to the sea, she says

Shall we go there, she says

Yes, why not, Asle says

and then they walk along side by side and Alida points

and says that over there is the Knoll, where you can see the sea, and when you're on the Knoll you can't see Leitet and the houses there and that's good, she says

You don't have any brothers or sisters, Alida says

No, Asle says

I have a sister, her name's Oline, Alida says

But I don't like my sister Oline, she says

And you have both a ma and a dad, she says

Yes, Asle says

I had both a ma and a dad, but then my dad went away and then he was gone and that was many years ago, Alida says

No one knows what happened to him, she says

Yes, Asle says

He just disappeared, Alida says

and they walk up the Knoll and they sit down on a big flat rock that lies there

Shall I tell you something, Alida says

Yes, Asle says

When you played, she says

Yes, Asle says

When you played I heard my dad singing, Alida says

Always, when I was little, he sang for me, she says

And that's the only thing I remember of my Pa Aslak, she says

I remember his voice, she says

And his voice was so like your playing, she says, and then she sits closer to Asle and they sit like that without saying anything

So you're Alida, he says

Yes I'm Alida and what about it, she says

and then she laughs a little and then she says that she

was only three when Pa Aslak disappeared never to come back and that the memory of his singing is the only memory she has of him, and she doesn't understand it, she says, but when she heard Asle play she heard Pa Aslak's voice in his playing, she says, and then she puts her head on Asle's shoulder and then she begins to cry and she puts her arms around Asle and she leans against him and Alida sits there close to Asle and cries and he doesn't quite know what to say or what to do, what he should do with his hands, what he should do with himself and then he puts his arms around Alida and he holds her tight and they sit there and feel each other and they feel that they hear the same thing and they feel that they are now soaring together and are together in the soaring and Asle feels that he cares much more about Alida than about himself and that he wants to give her everything that is good in the world

You must come down to the Boathouse tomorrow, Asle says

And then I can play more for you there, he says

We can sit on the bench outside the Boathouse and I can play for you, he says

And Alida says that she'll do that

And afterward we can come up here, to our Knoll, she says

and Asle and Alida stand up and they stand there and look down and then they only just glance at each other and they take each other's hands and then they just stand there

And out there is the sea, Alida says

It's great to see the sea, Asle says

and then they don't say anything and everything is settled and there is nothing that either has to be or should be said, everything is said anyway and everything is settled anyway

You're playing and my father's singing, Alida says

And Asle starts and wakes up and he looks at Alida

What did you say, Asle says

and Alida wakes up and looks at Asle

Did I say something, she says

No perhaps you didn't say anything, Asle says

Not that I know of, Alida says

Are you cold, Asle says

A little, Alida says

No I don't think I said anything, she says

I heard you say something about your father, but perhaps that was just something I dreamed, Asle says

Something about my father, Alida says

Yes I think I was dreaming, she says

You were dreaming, Asle says

Yes, Alida says

It was summer, she says

It was warm, she says

And I heard you playing, you were sitting there on the bench in front of the Boathouse playing and it was so nice to listen to, and then my dad came and he was singing and you were playing, she says

We must get up and go, Asle says

We can't sit here and sleep, he says

Have you been sleeping too, she says

Yes, I think I nodded off, he says

and Asle gets up

We must find some shelter, he says

and then Alida gets up too and they stand there and then Asle lifts the bundles and hangs them over his shoulders

We have to keep going, he says

But where, she says

There seems to be something they call an inn down the street here, on the other side of the street, and it seems we can get a room there, Asle says.

And the street here's supposed to be called Inste Street, yes, he says

and Alida lifts up her bags and then she stands there, Alida, with her long black hair all wet, hanging down over her breasts and her black eyes shining in the darkness and with her big stomach, she stands there, and she looks calmly at Asle and he bends down and picks up the fiddle case and then they begin to walk slowly along the street in the dark and the cold and the rain, now in late autumn, and they cross the street

There, above the door there, it says Inn, Asle says

Yes look at that, Alida says

and Asle goes and opens the door and he looks at Alida

Come now, he says

and Alida walks slowly forward and she walks past Asle and into the house and Asle walks in after her and he glimpses a man in the darkness in there, he is sitting at a table and on the table there is a lamp

Welcome, the Man says

and he looks at them

Do you have a room for us, Asle says

That should be possible, the Man says, and he looks at them and his eyes rest on Alida's stomach

Oh thank you, Asle says

and the Man is still looking at Alida's stomach

Yes, perhaps that's possible, the Man says

Thank you, thank you, Asle says

and the Man is still looking at Alida's stomach

Let's see, the Man says

and Alida looks at Asle

For how long, the Man says

We don't know, Asle says

It could be for a few days, the Man says

Yes, Asle says

You've just arrived in Bjørgvin, the Man says

and he's looking at Alida

And where from, the Man says

From Dylgja, Asle says

Ah, from Dylgja, the Man says

I suppose you can rent a room then, he says

Because you look so wet and cold, you can't walk through the streets in this cold night, and it's raining, and it's late autumn too, he says

Thank you, Asle says

and the Man leans over the book on the table in front of him and Alida looks urgently at Asle and then she takes his arm and he doesn't understand anything so she pulls at him as she begins to walk out and Asle follows and the Man looks up from the book and he says so they won't be staying there after all then, but if they realize that they have to find somewhere to stay, yes, they can come back, he says, and Alida opens the door and Asle holds the door open and they walk out and then they stand there in the street and then Alida says that they can't stay there, in that inn, didn't he notice anything, didn't he notice the eyes of that man who was sitting there, didn't he notice what those eyes said, doesn't he see anything, doesn't he notice anything, is she the only one who can see, Alida says, and Asle doesn't understand what she means

But you're so tired, you're wet and cold, and I must find shelter for you, Asle says Yes, Alida says

and then Asle and Alida begin to walk slowly down Inste Street in the rain and they arrive at an open square and they keep going, and then they come to a corner and they can see Vågen there at the opening at the end of the street and they go down the street and there they can see the Wharf and then there's an old woman walking in front of them, and Asle didn't notice her before, but now he can see her walking there in front of them, she bends against the wind and the cold and the rain, and she keeps walking, and where did she come from, it was like she appeared there all of a sudden, and she must have come out from a side street ahead of them and he didn't see her, that's what must have happened

That woman ahead of us, where did she come from, Alida says

I was thinking the same thing, Asle says

Suddenly she was just there, he says

Yes I suddenly just saw her there ahead of us in the street, Alida says

You're so tired, so tired, Asle says

Yes, Alida says

and the old woman there ahead of them stops and she takes out a large key and she puts it into a lock and then she unlocks the door to a small house there in the darkness and then she walks through the door and Asle says he thinks that's the first house where they asked for shelter, and Alida says yes she thinks it is and Asle hurries over and grabs the door handle and pulls the door open

Do you have a room for us, he says

and the Woman turns slowly to Asle and water is

running from her shawl and down her face and she holds
a lamp up to Asle's face

No is that you again, the Woman says

You already asked earlier today, she says

And don't you remember what I said, she says

Do you have a bad memory, she says

A room for you, she says

Yes we need a room for the night, Asle says

I don't have a room for you, says the Woman

How often must I tell you, she says

and Asle stands there and holds the door open and he
nods to Alida and she comes and stands in the doorway

So it's the two of you who need a room, the Woman says

I can understand that, she says

You should've thought about that before, she says

Before you behaved like that, she says

We can't walk around all night, Asle says

No who can do that in late autumn in this rain, the
Woman says

Not now, not in this rain and in this cold, she says

Not now in Bjørgvin in late autumn, she says

And we have nowhere to go, Alida says

You should've thought about that before, the Woman
says

But you didn't think then, did you, she says, and she
looks at Alida

Something else was bothering you then, she says

I've seen too many like you in my life, she says

I've often had them in my house, she says

And you think I should give you a room, she says

I should give a room to you and your bastard kid, she
says

What kind of person do you think I am, she says

You think I'm like that, me, she says

No, be on your way, she says

And the Woman hits out with her free arm to chase
them away

But, Asle says

No but, the Woman says

and she looks at Alida

I've had too many like you in my house already, the
Woman says

Girls like you, she says

Girls like you don't deserve anything better than walking around in the cold, there's nothing else for it, she says

Imagine behaving like such a fool, she says

Imagine not stopping to think, she says

and Asle puts a hand on Alida's shoulder and guides
her into the hall and then he closes the door behind her

Now listen here, the Woman says

Now imagine me having to go through this too, Jesus
Christ, she says

and Asle puts the bundles and the fiddle case down in
the hallway and then he goes to the Woman and he takes
the candleholder and he loosens the Woman's grip and
then he stands there and holds the candle up to Alida

You'll pay for this, the Woman says

Let me by, she says

and Asle blocks her way

Go inside, he says

and Asle opens one of the doors there in the hallway
and holds the candle up in the room

Go into the kitchen, he says

and Alida stands there

Do it, go into the kitchen, Asle says

and Alida walks through the open door and she sees
that there's an unlit lamp on the table over there by the
window and she walks over to the table, she puts her bags
down on the table and then she lights the lamp and she sits
down on a chair at the table and she looks at the open door
and she sees Asle standing there in the hallway holding his
hands over the Woman's mouth and then Asle closes the
door and Alida stretches out her legs under the table and
she breathes heavily several times and then she holds her
hands around the flames of the candle and it warms her,
it warms her so nicely that a sudden happiness spreads
through her arms and legs, and tears come to her eyes
and she sits and looks into the flame and she is so tired,
so tired, and she is so cold, so cold, and then Alida slowly
stands up and she takes the candle with her and she walks
over to the stove and she sees that there is wood in a box
by the stove and she puts some wood into the stove and
lights it and she stands there by the stove and she is so tired
that she hardly knows where she is and she is hungry, but
they have food, a lot of food, and soon she'll eat something
and gradually the stove will begin to warm them and she
holds her arms above the stove and she breathes heavily
again and then she sees that there is a bench along the wall
and then she walks over to the bench and there is a jacket
and a wool blanket on the bench and she pulls the jacket
over her head and then wraps herself in the blanket and
then she lies down and she closes her eyes and she hears
the rain out there in the street and then she blows out the
candle and she hears a squeaking, as if from a wheel, and
it is the sound of wheels striking against cobblestones out
there in the street and she sees the mist lifting and then the

sun breaks through and the sea lies there in front of her,
calm and glittering, and then she sees Asle walking along
out there in the street and he's pulling a wagon behind
him and there are a couple of barrels on the wagon and
Alida puts her hand on the thick black hair of the child
standing next to her and she tousles his hair and she says
you're my good boy Sigvald, and she sings a song to the
little boy, to little Sigvald, one of the songs Pa Aslak used
to sing to her, she now sings to little Sigvald, her little boy,
and he looks at her with his large black eyes and where
the fjord opens out to the sea she can see a boat with a
tall, straight mast drifting on the calm and glittering sea,
for there isn't a breath of wind in the air, and then she's a
bright star vanishing into the darkness and disappearing
and disappearing and then she hears a voice and she opens
her eyes and she sees Asle standing there

Were you asleep, he says

Yes, I think I fell asleep, Alida says

and she sees Asle standing there at the bench with a
candle in his hand and in the flame all she can see is his
black eyes and in his eyes she sees the voice of Pa Aslak
when he sang to her, when she was a little girl, before he
disappeared and was gone forever

Shall we have something to eat, Asle says

I'm hungry, he says

I'm hungry too, Alida says

and she sits up on the edge of the bench and now it
has become warm in the kitchen, nice and warm, and the
blanket opens and then she sits there and her breasts fall
heavily over her big and round stomach and then she sees
Asle undressing and he sits down next to her and he puts
his arm around her shoulders and then they lie down and

they lie there next to each other with the blanket covering them both Just rest for a bit first, Asle says

You've hardly slept for a long time, Alida says

No, he says

You must be very tired, she says

Yes, Asle says

And hungry, you're hungry too, Alida says

Yes very hungry, he says

First rest for a bit, and then eat, he says

and Asle and Alida lie close to each other and hold each other and then Asle sees the boat sail forward so nicely and evenly, and over there, there's Bjørgvin, the houses in Bjørgvin town, now they'll be there very soon, now they're finally there, and he sees Alida sitting there in the front of the boat and everything's fine, and they've done it, now they've managed to come to Bjørgvin and now their life will begin and he sees Alida standing up and she stands, huge, in the front of the boat, and Asle feels that the way he's made, it's not himself who's important, it's the big soaring that is important, fiddle playing has taught him that, it's the fiddler's fate to know things like that, and to him, the big soaring is Alida.

II

ASLE AND ALIDA are lying on a bench in a kitchen in a small house on Inste Street in Bjørgvin, and they sleep and they sleep, they sleep and they sleep and Asle wakes up and opens his eyes and he looks out into the room and he doesn't understand at first where he is and he sees Alida lying there next to him, sleeping with her mouth open and then he remembers and it's cold and gray in the kitchen and he stands up and lights a lamp and then he remembers and remembers and he puts wood into the stove and stokes the fire and he gets back under the blanket with Alida and then he lies there close to Alida and he hears the stove crackle and hum and he hears the rain in the street and on the roof and he is hungry, but they did bring a lot of good food with them from Herdis's larder in Brotet and once it gets a bit warmer in the kitchen he'll get up and find some food, and then, later today, he'll go to the Market Place and to the Wharf and see if there's any work and surely it should be possible to find something to do, and get some income, and Asle looks at Alida and now she seems to be awake

You're awake, says Asle

49

Are you there, says Alida

Yes, yes I'm here, says Asle

That's good, Alida says

and they lie there looking around the room

and you've fired up the stove, Alida says

Yes, yes, Asle says

and then they lie there silently and then Asle asks if he should go and find something to eat and Alida says yes that'd be good and then Asle goes and gets some food and then they sit up and they sit there and eat and then they get up, and their clothes are dry now, and they get dressed, and then they unpack everything that they brought with them in two bundles from the Boathouse in Dylgja.

Have you had a look around the house, Alida says

No, Asle says

and then Alida opens the nearest door and when Asle walks in with the lamp he sees it is a small living room, with nice pictures on the wall, and a table and chairs, and there's a door there, and Alida opens the door and Asle walks in with the candle and they see that beyond the living room there is a small chamber with a bed, nicely made, and with a plaid on the bed

This is a nice little house, isn't it, Alida says

Yes, Asle says

Yes, a fine house, Alida says

and then she bends forward and she says that suddenly it hurts so much, so much, suddenly her stomach hurts like it's been hit, she says, her stomach hurts so much, she says, so perhaps, perhaps she's about to give birth, she says, and she gives Asle a frightened look and he holds her around her shoulders and helps her into the bed there in the chamber and he pulls the blanket over her and Alida bends over and screams and twists and she manages to say that she's about to give birth now and Asle has to find someone who can come and help

Help, he says

I'm about to give birth, she says

You've got to get help, she says

Yes, Asle says

and he sees that Alida is lying there calmly now, the way she usually does

I'm about to give birth and you must get someone who can help, she says

Who, Asle says

I don't know, Alida says

But you must find someone, she says

There has to be someone who can help me in this big town of Bjørgvin, she says

Yes, Asle says

Someone who can help, yes, he says

and then Alida screams and twists and contorts her body there in bed and who, who can he ask, he doesn't know anyone in Bjørgvin, no one in the whole city of Bjørgvin and once more Alida is lying there calmly and the way she usually is

You must go and get someone, Alida says

and once more she screams and she lifts herself up so her stomach raises up there under the plaid

Yes, yes right away, Asle says

And he walks out into the kitchen and out into the hallway and he walks out into the street and it's gray and semi-dark out there in Inste Street and it rains and there's no one in sight, but he must find someone who can help Alida and he walks down the street and he should probably

walk to the end of the street and then go down to the
Market Place, because he should be able to find someone
there and he has come to the end of the street and he looks
toward the Market Place and there, ahead of him, walking
toward him, he sees the man he saw yesterday, the one
with the stick and the tall hat and the bearded face, the
one with the long black coat, just a few meters ahead of
him he sees the Man come walking toward him and surely
he can just ask him for help and he walks over to the Man
and looks at him

You, Asle says

Yes, the Man says

Can you, Asle says

Yes, the Man says

Can you help me, Asle says

Perhaps I can help you, the Man says

My wife's about to give birth, Asle says

I can't help with that, the Man says

But do you know where I can find help, Asle says

and the Man just stands there saying nothing

Yes there's an old woman up the street, he says

She's supposed to know about things like that, he says

We'll have to ask her, he says

and then the Man begins to walk up Inste Street with
slow short steps, he walks forward slowly and with dignity
while he moves the stick forward for each second step and
Asle walks a little behind him and he sees that the Man
is walking toward the small house where Alida now lies
in the chamber and screams and twists and then the Man
stops in front of the house where Asle and Alida found
shelter from the rain and the wind and the darkness late
in autumn and the Man knocks on the door and he stands

there and waits and then he turns to Asle and says that
she doesn't seem to be at home, the Young Midwife, and
then he knocks once more and he stands there and waits

No, the Man says

The Young Midwife doesn't seem to be at home, he says

There's got to be someone else, he says

Yes there's another Midwife out in Skutevika, he says

Yes, he says

Go to the Market Place, go out to the Wharf, and then
keep going until you come to Skutevika, and then you'll
have to ask for directions there, the Man says

and Asle nods and thanks him and turns and he walks
along the street again and he goes to the Market Place and
he crosses the Market Place and he goes to the Wharf and
then he walks along the Wharf and it's raining and it's cold
and Asle walks and he finds Skutevika and he is told where
he can find the Old Midwife's house and he knocks on her
door and she opens the door and she says oh well she'll
have to come with him and then she comes with him and
they walk to the little house there in Inste Street

So your wife's at the house of the Young Midwife, the
Old Midwife says

But if the Young Midwife can't help, then I can't help
either, she says

And Asle opens the door and he lights a lamp and he
opens the door to the living room and the Old Midwife
walks into the living room

Is she in the chamber, the Old Midwife says

and Asle nods and says yes and it's all quiet in there
now, there's no sound from the chamber

You stay here, the Old Midwife says

and she takes the lamp and she goes and opens the door

to the chamber and she walks in and she closes the door
behind her and everything is silent, as silent as only the
calm sea can be and time passes and time stands still and
nothing can be heard from the chamber and then Asle
hears a knock on the door and he walks into the hallway
and opens the door and he sees the man with the tall hat
and the bearded face and the long stick and the long coat
standing there

So here you are, the Man says

Yes, Asle says

My wife's giving birth, he says

But the Young Midwife wasn't at home, the Man says
and Asle doesn't know what to say

It's not her, it's the Old Midwife who's here, he says

I don't understand, the Man says

and they hear a terrible scream, as if the earth was opening, and then several more screams and the Man shakes
his head and then he walks slowly up Inste Street and Asle
walks out and he walks down Inste Street and he walks out
into the Market Place and he walks out along the Wharf
and he walks and walks, and he walks back to the Market
Place and then Asle hurries up Inste Street again and he
goes into the little house there and the Old Midwife is
sitting at the table in the kitchen

Yes now you've become a father, she says

You have a fine boy, she says

and she opens the door to the chamber and she stands
there and looks at Asle

But do you know where the Young Midwife is, the Old
Midwife says

No, Asle says

But now you must come into the chamber, she says

and Asle walks into the chamber and there in the bed
lies Alida and in the crook of her arm lies a little bundle
with black hair

So now little Sigvald is born, Asle says

and he sees that Alida nods

Now little Sigvald has entered this world, Asle says

and Asle looks at little Sigvald who opens his eyes and
a black and shining gleam comes toward him

Little Sigvald, yes, Alida says

and Asle stands there and time passes and it doesn't pass
and then he hears the Old Midwife say that she should
get back to Skutevika, they don't need her here anymore
and Asle just stands there and he looks at Alida and she
lies there and looks and looks at little Sigvald and then
Asle walks over and lifts up little Sigvald and holds him
up in the air

Yes indeed, Asle says

No there's only us left, Alida says

You and me, Asle says

And then little Sigvald, Alida says

Olav's Dreams

HE WALKS ALONG the bend and once he's around the bend he'll be able to see the fjord, Olav thinks, for now he is Olav, not Asle, and now Alida is not Alida, but Åsta, now they are Åsta and Olav Vik, Olav thinks, and he thinks that today he has to go to Bjørgvin and do his errand there and he has rounded the bend and now he sees that the fjord is glittering, only now does he see it, because today the fjord is glittering, yes sometimes the fjord glitters, and when it glitters the mountains are reflected in the fjord and beyond the reflections the fjord is amazingly blue, and the fjord's blue glittering meets almost imperceptibly with the white and blue of the sky, Olav thought, and he sees a man ahead of him on the road, quite far ahead of him, but who is it, does he recognize the man, perhaps he has seen him before, there was something about the way he walked, stooped, but was he sure he had seen him before, no, that he wasn't, and why was this man walking here along the road in Barmen, because there was never anyone here, and then suddenly there he was, the man, and now he was walking ahead of him on the road and the man wasn't big, but quite small, and the man was wearing black and he walked slowly and a little stooped, with unhurried steps, stooped, that's how he walked, as if he was walking and thinking, perhaps, that's how he walked, and on his head he wore a gray knit cap, and why is he walking so slowly,

for he must be walking slowly because Olav is getting closer
and closer no matter how slowly he walks, and he doesn't
want to walk slowly, he wants to walk as fast as he possibly
can, he wants to walk to Bjørgvin and do what he has to
do there and then he wants to walk home again as fast as
he possibly can, to Åsta and little Sigvald, but can he just
pass the man like it was nothing, can he, and he probably
must, Olav thinks, and even if he walks as slowly as he can
he keeps getting closer and closer to the man, and why did
the man come here, no one ever came here, not once since
they lived in Barmen did anyone come here, so why was
the man walking there ahead of him on the road, like an
obstacle, because if he'd walked steadily at his usual pace,
he would have overtaken the man a long time ago, and it
would've taken a much shorter time if he'd walked as fast as
he could the way he'd like to, then he would've overtaken
the man, and then he would've had to overtake the man,
and he would've had to pass him and that, to pass him, no
that he didn't want, because then the man would look at
him and perhaps the man would talk to him too and perhaps he would recognize him, because perhaps he knew
the man, or had met him before, that could be, or at least
perhaps the man knew him, even if he didn't know the
man the man might know him, yes of course, and perhaps
it was him the man had come here for, perhaps the man
had come here to find him, perhaps it was to look for him
that the man was walking along here, he was on his way
from somewhere, where he had been looking for him, and
to somewhere else, where he was also going to look for
him, and suddenly, Olav thinks, that's what it feels like,
that it's him the man is after, and why, why was the man
looking for him, what could it be, and why did the man

walk so slowly, Olav thinks, and he begins to walk even
more slowly and he looks at the fjord and he sees that it is
glittering and blue, and why was this man walking ahead
of him on a day when the fjord finally glitters, a black man,
a small man, a stooped man, a man with a gray knit cap,
and what does the man want with him, it probably can't be
anything good, but it can't be like that, because of course
the man doesn't want anything with him, why would the
man come here to look for him, why is he thinking like
that, what's he thinking, Olav thinks, and if only the man
doesn't turn around and look at him, because he doesn't
want the man to notice him, but the man is walking so
slowly and then he too must walk slowly, and then the
man stops, and then Olav stops too, and he can't just stand
there like that, he's on his way to Bjørgvin, and he wants
to walk as fast as he can straight to Bjørgvin and do his
errand and then walk home again, and so he can't stand
there like that and look at a man on the road in front of
him, rather than standing there like this he should start to
run, perhaps he should take a running leap and run straight
past the man, and if the man shouted at him, he wouldn't
answer, he would just run as fast as he could, run past him,
past the man, because he can't keep standing like this, and
walking like this, so slowly, he who never walked like this,
never, he always walked steadily forward, unless he ran,
because that happened too, he sometimes ran, but it didn't
happen all that often, no I can't do this, Olav thought, and
then he starts to walk the way he usually walks, steadily,
and he comes closer and closer to the man and is side by
side with the man, and when he is next to the man, the
man looks at him and he sees that it is an old man, and
the Old Man stops

Well look here it's that fellow, the Old Man says

and he breathes heavily

Yes it's that fellow, he says

and Olav just keeps going, because there was something familiar with the Old Man, but where had he seen him before, was it in Dylgja, in Bjørgvin, at least he hadn't seen him here in Barmen, he was sure of that, because here there was never anyone, at least he hadn't seen anyone before today

Yes that fellow, the Old Man says

and Olav keeps going and doesn't turn around, because it seems like the Old Man recognizes him

Don't you recognize me, the Old Man says

Hello there Asle, he says

I want to talk to you, he says

I have something to ask you, he says

I could almost say it's because of you I'm walking here, he says

Me, you recognize me, don't you, he says

Asle wait, he says

Stop Asle, he says

Surely you remember me, he says

Don't you remember the last time we met, he says

Surely you remember me, he says

Yes you do, he says

Stop now and talk to me, because I've come here to see you, he says

I took a trip to look for you, for you both, yes to be honest, he says

and Olav tries all he can to remember who the Old Man could be, and why he says Asle, and that he has come to talk to Asle, and Olav walks as fast as he can and he

thinks that he must get away from the Old Man, because
what does he want with him, but run, no he doesn't want
to run, he'll just walk, and he'll walk as fast as he can,
because the Old Man, he walks so slowly, with unhurried
steps, and he said that he had come here to look for him,
for them, Olav thinks, and if that's what he says, it must
be true, or perhaps it's just something he says to scare him,
something he says to have a hold over him, and how can
he know his name, he thinks, but the Old Man is so small,
and so stooped, so he could always handle him, if need
be, Olav thinks

Now look what a hurry this fellow's in, says the Old
Man

Wait, he says

and he almost shouts after Olav, and his voice is thin,
there's a squeaky sound in his voice when he shouts and
Olav just keeps walking and he thinks no, no way will he
answer, he's not going to answer, he thinks

Yes my word, the Old Man says

and Olav thinks, no he won't turn around, because now
he is already quite a ways ahead of the Old Man and now,
now he's just walking at his normal pace, steadily, he walks
steadily, he'll keep walking, he thinks, and then he turns
his head, just briefly, just for a second

Talk about being in a hurry, the Old Man says

Wait, wait, he says

Don't you remember me, he says

Don't you recall, he says

Ha, no you don't seem to, he says

Surely you must remember me, he says

Stop then, he says

Stop Asle, he says

and he says it in a loud voice, and he almost shouts it
with this awful squeaking and whining in his voice and
Olav stops and he turns toward the Old Man

Don't meddle, Olav says

No, no, the Old Man says

But don't you remember me, he says

No, Olav says

No, well, you're a fine one, says the Old Man

and at that moment Olav felt a jolt and he tore himself
loose and he turned away from the Old Man and then,
Olav thought, then things were wrong again, he thinks, it
is always like this, and why does he say this, that the Old
Man shouldn't meddle, why does he always say things like
that, what's wrong with him, why can't he say it as it is,
say it properly, why is he like that, Olav thinks, and he
suddenly feels so different, he sees differently, perhaps, or
he hears differently, perhaps, or whatever it is and that
Old Man, who could that be, Olav thinks, and he turns
around and where is the Old Man, he was right there, he
talked to him, he saw him there just now, didn't he, yes,
yes of course he did, but where is he now, he can't have
disappeared into thin air, Olav thinks and he keeps walking, he walks on because he is going to Bjørgvin now and
there he will do his errand and then he'll come home again
to Åsta and little Sigvald, and then, when he is back home
again, they will put the rings on their fingers and then,
even if they are not married, at least it will look like they
are, because he still has the money he got for the fiddle
and they're going to buy rings for them, the money was
put aside for that, yes now, now on this fine day, on this
day when the fjord is glittering blue, he'll walk to Bjørgvin
and there he'll buy rings and then he'll walk back home

again to Åsta and little Sigvald and then he'll never leave them again, Olav thinks and without thinking about anything else, just about Åsta, about the ring he'll put on her finger, he keeps walking, that's all he's thinking about as he walks and then he has arrived in Bjørgvin and he walks down a street, a street he hasn't been in before, and there, right ahead of him, he sees that the street ends in a door, there's a door a few meters ahead of him and he walks up to the door, it's brown and heavy, and he opens the door and walks into a dark hallway where the wooden logs lie heavily on top of each other and he hears voices, and at the end of the hallway he sees light, and he hears voices, many voices talking all at once so there's a heavy clamor of voices and he continues along the hallway and into the light and he sees faces half lit by lamps and half concealed by smoke and he sees eyes and teeth and hats and heads and they sit at tables, the hats and the heads, tightly together, and suddenly laughter rings out between the walls and a few are standing at a counter and one of them turns around and looks straight at him and Olav sneaks past a couple of tables and then they stand tightly together in front of him and he stands there and can't get anywhere and now more and more people are standing behind him, so he just has to stand there, if he's going to get over to the counter and get a tankard he must be patient, he thinks, but it should be all right, he thinks, because it's not too bad in here, there's light and laughter here, Olav thinks, and he stands there and no one notices him standing there, everyone is busy with their own things, talking to someone else, and all the clamoring of the voices, and one voice cannot be separated from another voice, and not one face from another face, all the voices are like one jabbering voice and all the faces like

one face and then someone turns around and he's wearing
a gray knit cap on his head and holding a tankard in his
hand and it's the man who was walking ahead of him when
he was in Barmen this morning, and now he's there again,
the Old Man and he is walking toward Olav and he looks
straight into his face

But there you are, the Old Man says

I arrived before you, didn't I, he says

I know the way better than you, he says

I took a shortcut, he says

Ha, he says

You walked fast, yes, he says

But I got here faster, he says

And I, I knew where I would find you, obviously, he says

Of course I knew you were going to Skjenkjestova, that
was obvious, he says

You can't trick me, he says

You don't trick an old man that easily, he says

I know people like you, he says

and the Old Man lifts the tankard to his mouth and
drinks and then he wipes his mouth

That's how it is, he says

and Olav sees there's some space in front of him and he
moves forward and he feels a prickle in his back

So now you've got to have a tankard, the Old Man
says and Olav thinks that he mustn't answer, he won't say
a single word

Yes, of course you do, the Old Man says

That's just what you need, he says

and another man in front of Olav turns around and he
holds a tankard tightly to his chest and he makes room
for Olav and he stops and then he stands there holding

his tankard and he lifts the tankard to his mouth as Olav walks past him and a little closer to the counter

We'll talk later, the Old Man says

and he's right behind Olav

I'll just wait, he says

You get yourself a tankard, and then we'll talk, he says

I'll stay here in Skjenkjestova, he says

and Olav looks straight ahead and now there's only one person between him and the counter, but people are sitting shoulder to shoulder on benches around the counter and the man in front of Olav tries to push between two of them who are sitting there and then one of them grabs the shoulder of the man who wants to get to the counter and pushes him back and the man who wants to get to the counter grabs the shoulder of the man sitting there and then they stand there and hold each other and they say something to each other but Olav can't hear what they're saying and then they let go of each other and then the man who is sitting pulls back a little and the man who wants to get to the counter gets there and now Olav is next in line, he thinks, they don't waste any time, he thinks, now he too will get himself a tankard and then the man at the counter turns and almost shoves his tankard into Olav's chest as he turns and twists the tankard away from Olav and then he follows his arm and Olav gets to the counter and then he stands there and looks at one of the beer servers and Olav waves at him and the beer server lifts a tankard up to Olav and he puts it down in front of Olav and he finds a bill and gives it to the man who serves the beer and Olav gets a coin back and he picks up the tankard and he turns around with the tankard in his hand and now there are three, four in a row behind him and he moves a little to

the side and then he stands there and he lifts the tankard
to his mouth

Cheers, one of them says

and Olav looks up and he sees the Old Man clink his
tankard against his tankard

Can't say there's much strength in you, the Old Man
says

But once you've had a drink, it'll get better, he says

I can wait, he says

So who are you, someone else says

And Olav turns to the side and looks into a long face
under almost white hair, although the man standing there
can't be much older than Olav

Me, Olav says

Yes, the other says

Who am I, Olav says

You've just arrived, the other man says

and Olav looks at him

Yes I'm just passing through Bjørgvin, Olav says

Me too, the other man says

Have you been here before, Olav says

No, no this is the first time, the other man says

I'm from the northern country, he says

I arrived here yesterday, and Bjørgvin, yes you can't find
a bigger and better city, he says

You came on a boat, Olav says

Yes, on the skiff Elisa, fully loaded, he says

Fully loaded with the finest and driest fish, he says

And well paid for the fish, yes we were well paid, he says

Not a bad word about that shopkeeper, he says

And now you'll be staying in Bjørgvin for a few days,
Olav says

And then I'll be going home again, the other man says and he puts his hand in his pocket and he pulls out a bracelet of the yellowest gold and the bluest of blue pearls, the finest thing Olav has ever seen

This is what she'll get, he says

and he holds the bracelet up in front of Olav

My woman at home, the woman I'm engaged to, he says

Oh that's a fine bracelet, Olav says

and he thinks that a thing like that, that's what he too must buy for Åsta, yes, he thinks

My Nilma, the other man says

because think how nice such a bracelet would look on Åsta's arm, Olav thinks

She and I are engaged, yes, Nilma and I, he says

And now, yes, everything I've earned I've spent on buying her this bracelet, he says

and Olav can see it so clearly, as if he were actually looking at it, Åsta's arm with the bracelet, he must get one like it, yes, he has gone to Bjørgvin to buy rings, so it can look l like they're married, him and Åsta, but what's a ring against a bracelet like that, yes, yes, he'll come home to Åsta with such a bracelet, Olav thinks, and the other man puts the bracelet back in his pocket and he holds out his hand

Åsgaut, he says

My name's Åsgaut, he says

And my name's Olav, Olav says

You're not from Bjørgvin either, from what I hear, Åsgaut says

No, no, Olav says

I come from a place further north from here, he says

Where, Åsgaut says

It's called Vik, Olav says

So you come from Vik, Åsgaut says

Yes, Olav says

But where can you buy such a thing, he says

The bracelet, Åsgaut says

Yes, Olav says

I bought mine at a stall down by the Wharf, there were all sorts of things there, yes, it's incredible what you can get there, I didn't think you could find so much finery in the whole wide world, Åsgaut says

Do you want to buy a bracelet too, he says

Yes, yes I do, Olav says

But it's expensive, Åsgaut says

And very nice, Olav says

Nice, oh yes, Åsgaut says

and Olav thinks that he'll just finish his drink and leave and walk over to the stall at the Wharf because Åsta is going to have a bracelet like that, that's for sure, he thinks

Were there more bracelets like that left, he says

One more, I think, Åsgaut says

and Olav lifts the tankard to his mouth and drinks and he puts the tankard down and then he looks straight into the Old Man's face, his squinting eyes, his narrow mouth

So you're from Vik, are you, the Old Man says

I'll tell you where you're from, he says

I'm from Vik, yes, Olav says

Since you, Asle, don't want to say where you're from, I'll say it, the Old Man says

I'm not Asle, says Olav

Aren't you, the Old Man says

No, Olav says

But I know, I know his name and where he comes from, because he told me, Åsgaut says

I know that his name's Olav, he says

And that he's from Vik, he says

So he is, is he, the Old Man says

Yes, yes he knows it already, I've told him, Olav says

Say where you're from, the Old Man says

and Olav doesn't answer

You're from Dylgja, the Old Man says

Me, I'm from Måsøy, Åsgaut says

From Måsøy, up north, he says

Someone has to be from Måsøy, from way up north, everybody can't be from Bjørgvin because then no one can travel here with fish, with the finest, driest fish, he says

Oh yes he is, he's from Dylgja, the Old Man says

His name's Asle and he's from Dylgja, he says

and they just stand there and don't say anything

Well cheers then, Åsgaut says and he lifts his tankard

and the Old Man holds his tankard in front of his chest and squints at Olav

Cheers, Olav says

and he lifts his tankard up to Åsgaut's tankard and they clink

You won't clink with me, the Old Man says

No, no, you do what you like, he says

and they all lift their tankards to their mouths and drink

Dylgja, yes, the Old Man says

And a man was killed there, isn't that so, he then says

You don't say, Olav says

No I didn't know that, he says

Who was it, he says

I think it was a fisherman who lived in a boathouse,
the Old Man says

And then, he says

Yes and then a woman was found dead as well, and after
that the daughter disappeared, he says

and he looks at Olav

There was someone called Asle who lived there in the
boathouse before the man who was killed came there, the
Old Man says

It was you who lived there, before that fisherman came
there, he says

and Olav sees the Old Man empty his tankard, satisfied

And strangely enough, yes, just around the same time,
an old woman disappeared here in Bjørgvin, and she was
never found, a midwife, the Old Man says

Someone I knew well, he says

and he dries his mouth and turns to the counter and
Olav stands there and he looks down into this tankard
and he hears Åsgaut ask if it's been a long time since he's
been home

Yes, several years, Olav says

Yes, that's often how it goes, Åsgaut says

Once you go away, yes, many years can pass before you
get back home again, he says

And if it hadn't been for Nilma, I suppose I'd have stayed
in Bjørgvin too, in such a great and grand city, he says

and then Åsgaut once more takes out the bracelet of the
yellowest gold and the bluest of blue pearls and he stands
there and holds it up between himself and Olav and they
both look at it

You should buy one like it too, Åsgaut says

Oh yes, I will, Olav says

Yes, you must, if you have the money, Åsgaut says

Yes, Olav says

and he sees that there isn't much left in the tankard and he lifts it to his mouth and empties it and he sees the Old Man standing in front of him with a full tankard in his hand

So you won't be going home, the Old Man says

Home, Olav says

Yes, to Dylgja, the Old Man says

I'm not from Dylgja, Olav says

You don't have any family there, the Old Man says

No, Olav says

Oh well then, the Old Man says

Yes, in Dylgja, a man was killed there, yes, he says

and the Old Man lifts his tankard to his mouth again and drinks

Who killed him, Olav says

Who knows, the Old Man says

and he squints at Olav

Who could it have been, he said

You wouldn't know anything about it, would you, he says

and Olav doesn't answer

But they haven't caught him, the killer, Olav says

No, no, not that I know, the Old Man says

No they haven't found him, he says

What a terrible thing, Olav says

Yes, a terrible business, the Old Man says

and then they stand there without saying anything and Olav can see that there's not much left in the tankard and he thinks that he'll drink slowly, but why would he do that, he thinks, and why did he go into Skjenkjestova in the first place, he had nothing to do here, why stand here in this clamor of voices, and then that Old Man, he'll soon start talking again, so he should just finish his drink and then he should get out of there, because now he must go directly to the stall on the Wharf and buy the bracelet for Åsta, the ring can wait till later, he thinks, no, he'll do it right away, but does he have enough money, he thinks, no, no he's sure he doesn't, then how can he get the bracelet, and then he hears the Old Man saying yes, Asle, well yes I can understand that you don't want to go back to Dylgja, he says

My name isn't Asle, Olav says

and he hears the Old Man saying that no, no it isn't, of course his name isn't Asle, he says

No my name is Olav, Olav says

So your name's Olav, the Old Man says

Olav, yes, Olav says

Yes Olav's my name, too, the Old Man says

I'm the one who's called Olav, not you, he says

and he holds up his tankard to Olav

Me, he says

Yes, Olav says

Me, I've got family on Dylgja, yes I do, he says

Yes, Olav says

I was born there, he says

Yes, Olav says

On a small farm, yes, the farm is totally isolated there, he says

Yes, Olav says

And then I've been back there a few times too, yes, if not all that often, he says

Not all that often, no, he says

I'd rather stay here in Bjørgvin, he says

But the last time I was there, yes, then I heard about the evil deed someone had committed, he says

and he looks at Olav for a long time and then the Old Man moves his head from side to side, back and forth, and Olav thinks that now he must get away, why on earth is he here in Skjenkjestova, now he'll go to the stall on the Wharf and buy the bracelet of the yellowest gold with the bluest of blue pearls for Åsta, Olav thinks, and he hears the Old Man saying that he knows he's standing there chatting with a killer, but he's not going to tell anyone else, no he won't, why would he want Asle to be brought to justice, no not at all, why would he, he says, no, no, of course he won't, no he won't say anything, at least he won't say anything if Olav can give him a bill or two or three, or perhaps even buy him a tankard as well, he says

But of course it wasn't you, he says

Of course not, he says

Me, Olav says

The man they think is the killer, yes, his name's supposed to be Asle, the Old Man says

That's what they say in Dylgja, he says

The last time I was there, yes, that's what they said, he says

At least that's what they say, he says

Yes, that's what I was told the last time I was in Dylgja, he says

and Olav finishes his beer

I'm from Dylgja, yes I am, the Old Man says

I come from a small farm in Dylgja, yes, just rocky crags with a bit of swampy soil between them, yes, he says

But then there was the sea, and the fjord and the ocean and the fish, yes, he says

But where I grew up, no one lives there now, he says

That's how it turned out, he says

Because rocks and soggy soil can't feed many, no, he says

You couldn't live there, he says

Everyone had to leave, he says

The way you and I had to, he says

and Olav looks around and he's trying to find a place to put down his empty tankard, because he can't stay here, and why did he come here anyway, to Skjenkjestova, it's so crowded in here, and why is he standing there listening to the Old Man chattering away, and now he's standing there looking at him so strangely, and what does the Old Man want with him, no he mustn't stay here, of course not, Olav thinks

Can I buy you a tankard, the Old Man says

No thanks, I have to be on my way, Olav says

But you, yes, perhaps you can buy me one, the Old Man says

and Olav looks at him

I'm running a bit short at the moment, the Old Man says

Yes, I don't like to ask you for it, of course, he says

I almost feel ashamed, I do, he says

Yes, that I do, he says

I feel ashamed, but I've got a thirst, too, I can't deny that, he says

and Olav doesn't answer

You don't want to, the Old Man says

No I don't suppose you have much to spend either, he says

Not many people do, he says

Almost no one, he says

And everyone still spends and spends, they buy and buy, tankard after tankard, he says

I think I have to go, Olav says

and he hears Åsgaut say are you leaving and Olav says yes he must, he'll be going now to buy the bracelet of the yellowest gold and the bluest of blue pearls, he says, and Åsgaut asks if he knows where the stall is on the Wharf where they sell things like that and Olav says no he doesn't and Åsgaut says that if he wants he can show him where the stall is, because everyone's leaving Skjenkjestova now anyway, they're all going out the door, one after the other, he says, and Olav looks around and he sees that everyone is leaving Skjenkjestova, and he should leave himself, he too, like everyone else, he thinks

There are fewer and fewer people, Olav says

Yes so there are, the Old Man says

Everyone's leaving, he says

So they are, Olav says

That's strange, Åsgaut says

That everyone is suddenly leaving, he says

Yes, Olav says

Everyone's leaving, yes, the Old Man says

and Olav begins to walk toward the door and then a hand grabs his shoulder and he turns around and he looks into the Old Man's face, it's a face with small wet pale-red eyes, and he sees narrow moist lips quivering and making an open mouth

You're Asle, he says

And Olav feels cold where the Old Man has grabbed his shoulder and he wriggles loose from the hand that tries to hold him back but lets go and then he walks toward the

door and he hears the Old Man saying you're Asle, you're
Asle behind him and he mustn't answer, just walk out and
he opens the door and he goes out and then he stands there
in the street outside Skjenkjestova and then, he thinks, then
he'll go straight to the Wharf and he knows the way there,
he knows Bjørgvin that much, because he's been around
here quite a lot, although he can't claim that he's very familiar with the area, he hasn't lived in Bjørgvin after all, and not
everyone here in Bjørgvin tonight has done that, he thinks,
no, not at all, he thinks, there must be many who are here
for the first time, like Åsgaut, he thinks, but he, he's lived
here, so he'll find his way to the stall on the Wharf where
they sell the finest bracelets, and the rings can wait, for
Åsta's arm will be so lovely with such a bracelet on it, Olav
thinks, and he walks swiftly down toward Vågen and the
Wharf and then he hears someone shout wait behind him
and he turns around and he sees a girl with long fair hair
come walking swiftly along the street toward him

So it's you, the Girl says

Wait, she says

You were looking for me, I saw that, she says

Was I, Olav says

Yes, yes you were, she says

And it's good to see you again, she says

Do we know each other, Olav says

Don't you remember me, she says

Should I remember you, Olav says

Yes, yes don't you, she says

No, he says

You came and knocked on my door, she says

and the Girl laughs and nudges him

Did I, Olav says Yes, she says

I can't remember that, he says

You don't want to remember, she says

and she nudges him again and then she puts her arm in his arm

But then, then we couldn't talk, she says

No, he says

Why not, she says

And Olav begins to walk along the street and she holds on to his arm and follows

Because then you weren't alone, she says

Because then you were dragging that miserable wretch along, she says

A small dark one, yes, she says

You can spot them a mile off, she says

There are swarms of them here in Bjørgvin, she says

I don't know where they all come from, she says

As soon as one leaves two more arrive, she says

and she leans against this shoulder

But you used your brains and got rid of her, she says

And that I can understand, she says

If there's something I understand it's that, she says

I don't know you, Olav says

And now, now you're alone, she says

and the Girl leans her head on his shoulder

I don't know you, Olav says

You can get to know me, if you want to, the Girl says

Where do you live, she says

I don't live anywhere, he says

But I know of somewhere, she says

Because you've got money, don't you, she says

and they keep walking, she with her head against his shoulder

I don't have much, he says

But one or two bills surely, she says

and suddenly she tugs his arm and she pulls him with her between two houses, and it's narrow, so narrow that there is only just room for two in there between the houses, and she grabs his hand and then she walks further in, as far as she can into the alley, and it's totally dark there, and she stops

Here, she says

and she stands in front of him and she puts her arms around him and she pushes her breasts against his chest and she rubs her breasts against his chest

You can touch them, she says

and she kisses his cheek and then she licks the skin there with her tongue

I have to go now, he says

Oh, she says

and she lets go of him

There's something I have to do, he says

and he begins to walk out of the alley

All right then, she says

What an idiot, she says

The biggest idiot in Bjørgvin, she says

And she too begins to walk out of the alley

Couldn't you have said it from the beginning, she says

Before we went into the alley, she says

and they come out into the street

The biggest idiot in Bjørgvin, that's you, she says

and Olav thinks there's something he has to ask her, he has to say something to her, something or other, he thinks

Do you know where Øvste Street is, he says

Of course I do, she says

Just over there, she says

You walk along there and then up that way, she says and she points

No you can find it for yourself, she says

and Olav sees the Girl turn around and walk back up the street and he thinks that Øvste Street should be just over there, yes, and there, he even lived there, yes, he did, he and Åsta and Sigvald lived there, he thinks, they lived in that little house in Øvste Street and now that he's so close he might as well go take a look at the house, it would be nice to see it again, Olav thinks, and he walks along and then he arrives at where Øvste Street begins and he walks along Øvste Street and there, over there, there's the little house where he and Åsta lived and where little Sigvald was born and he stops and he sees himself standing in front of the house there in Øvste Street and next to him there are two bundles with everything they own, that was the last time he was here, Olav thinks, and he sees himself standing there and he sees Alida come out the door and she holds little Sigvald against her chest and he is well wrapped in a blanket, and then Alida stands in front of the house there in Øvste Street and she looks at the house

Do we have to leave now, she says

We've had such a good life here, she says

I've never felt as comfortable anywhere as I do here, she says

Can't we stay here, she says

I think we have to leave, Asle says

We have to say good-bye to the house, Alida says

Yes I think we do, Asle says

I've enjoyed my time here so much, Alida says

I don't want to leave the house, she says

But we must, Olav says

We can't stay in this house any longer, he says

Are you quite sure about that, Alida says

Yes, he says

But why, she says

That's just how it is, he says

It's not our house, he says

But no one else is living there, Alida says

The woman who lived here will come back, you'll see, Asle says

But it's been so long, Alida says

Someone will come, he says

That's not certain, she says

But it's her house, he says

Yes but since she hasn't come back, Alida says

She'll come, or perhaps someone else will come, someone or other, and then we won't be able to be there, Asle says

But it's been so long and no one has come, she says

Yes, he says

So then we can just stay here, she says

No, he says

It's not our house, of course, he says

But, she says

We have to leave now, he says

We've talked about this so often, he says

Yes, she says

We're going now, Asle says

and he lifts up the two bundles with everything they own and then they walk down the street, him in front, and Alida with little Sigvald to her breast right behind him

Wait, Alida says

and Asle stops

Where are we going, she says

and he doesn't answer

Where are we going, she says

We're not going to stay here in Bjørgvin, he says

But didn't we enjoy it here, Alida says

Yes, but we can't stay here any longer, Asle says

Why not, she says

I think someone's out to get us, he says

Someone's out to get us, she says

Yes I think they are, he says

How do you know that, she says

I just know, he says

and he says that they have to get away from Bjørgvin as fast as they possibly can, and once they've left Bjørgvin behind them, they can take it more calmly, then they can walk slowly, and it's summer and a warm day and they can enjoy themselves, and he did get a bit of money for the fiddle, so they have a little something to help them along, he says, and Alida says he shouldn't have sold the fiddle, because it was so lovely to listen when he sat there and played and he said that they really needed the money and besides he didn't want to live the life his father did, he didn't want to leave her and their child at home, he wanted to be with his family and not have to be with all the others, that wasn't good for anyone, what's good is to be with those you belong to, perhaps he was born with the fate of a fiddler, but he wanted to fight that fate, and that's why he sold the fiddle, he was no longer a fiddler, he had become a father now and he had become her husband, if not in the eyes of the law, then in reality, he says, that's how it is, and if that's how it is, then the fiddle isn't needed, and now that they really needed money, yes they may as well sell the fiddle, and now that the fiddle was sold there was nothing more to talk about, what's done is done, fiddle and everything else, Asle says and he says that they can't stand here and quarrel, she has to come now, they have to go now and Alida says that she was sure he was right to sell the fiddle, but he did play so lovely, so lovely, she said, and he doesn't answer and they begin to walk down the street and they keep walking and then they arrive at the Wharf and they walk along the Wharf and they don't say anything and they walk and walk and Olav thinks, as he stops and stands there, that he mustn't stand here like this, he's going to go to the stall on the Wharf and with the money he got for the fiddle he's going to buy the finest bracelet imaginable for Åsta, Olav thinks, and he begins to walk down toward the Wharf and he sees himself walking much farther along there on the Wharf and Alida is walking just behind him with little Sigvald at her breast and they don't say anything and the distance between the houses gets bigger and soon there's an even bigger distance between the houses and the day is far advanced and it's not warm and not cold, it's good walking weather and even if he's carrying a heavy load, it doesn't feel heavy because Alida is walking right behind him with little Sigvald against her breast and now and then the sun shines and now and then there are clouds and he doesn't know where they're going, and Alida doesn't know where they're going, but they have food with them, and they have clothes and a few other things they might need too

Where are we going, Alida says

I don't know, Asle says

We'll go to where we end up, she says

We'll go where the road leads us, he says

I'm a little tired, she says

Then we must rest, he says

and they stop and they stand and look around

Down there, on the ridge, we can rest there, she says

Yes we can, he says

and then they go and sit down on the ridge and they sit there and look out on the fjord, and the fjord is completely calm, nothing is moving out there, the fjord is glitteringly blue and Asle says that today the fjord is glittering and that doesn't happen very often, he says, and then they see a fish leap and he says that was probably a salmon and it was a big one, he says, and Alida says that this is where they should've lived and then he says that they cannot settle so close to Bjørgvin and she says why not and he says that they just can't, someone could find them and she says why does that matter and he says she must remember how they came to Bjørgvin and she says that thing about the boat and he says yes that too and then Alida says that she's hungry and Asle says that they have a whole cured leg of mutton, don't they, there's no lack of food, so no, they won't go hungry, he's taken care of that, he says, and Alida asks if he bought the leg of mutton and he says he didn't have to do that, but the meat seemed to be well cured, he says, and there, over there, she can hear what must be a brook, Alida says, so they won't go thirsty when they eat the salty meat, she says, and he unpacks the leg of mutton and then he holds it up in the air in one hand and he begins to swing it around up there in the air and she begins to laugh and she says that he mustn't do something like that, you shouldn't play with your food, she says, and Asle says that now she sounded just like her mother and she says oh dear, no not that, but

I suppose I too will end up like her, now that I've become a mother as well, I'll become like my own mother

Don't say that, he says

What I said just now, I must've learned from my own mother, she says

And I from my own mother, he says

and then she puts the bundle with little Sigvald down on the ridge and she sits down and then Asle sits down and he takes out the knife and then he cuts the leg of mutton to the bone and he cuts again and then he sits there with a thick slice in his hand and he hands the slice to Alida and she begins to chew the meat and she chews and says well this is nice, dry and nice and not too salty, she says, and he cuts a slice to himself and he tastes it and he says that it tastes good, no one can say otherwise, it was nice, meat cannot taste better, he says, and then Alida opens the pack of flatbread and the jar of butter and she spreads thick layers of butter over several slices of flatbread and he cuts some more meat and then they sit there and eat without saying anything

I'll go and get some water, Olav says

and he takes a flask and he hears the brook flowing and he walks toward the sound and then he sees a lovely fresh stream flowing down and down, from the mountain up there it flows downward, and the stream goes out into the fjord, and he fills his flask and with good cold water he walks back to Alida and he hands her the flask and she drinks and drinks and then she hands back the flask to him and he too drinks and drinks and then Alida says she is so glad that she has met him and he says that he is so glad that he has met her

The three of us, Alida says

You and me and little Sigvald, Asle says

The three of us, yes, he says

and Olav walks slowly along the Wharf and now he must go directly to the place where he can find the stall where they sell the finest bracelets in the world, he must manage to find the stall, and perhaps he can ask someone too, because there had to be someone who can tell him where that stall is, and there, ahead of him on the Wharf, he sees Åsgaut standing there smiling at him

You can't find the stall, Åsgaut says

I thought so, that you wouldn't find it, it's not so easy to find that stall, but I can help you, he says

Oh no, no, Olav says

The stall is difficult to find, Åsgaut says

But now, now I'll help you find it, he says

It's a bit further down the Wharf, and then up an alley, he says

I'll help you, he says

Thank you, Olav says

Verily I will, Åsgaut says

and Olav feels a joy flowing through him, for now, now he will buy the finest bracelet in the world, in the yellowest gold, with the bluest of blue pearls, and soon it will be around Åsta's arm, he thinks

I have a bit of money, yes, Olav says

He wants to sell, so perhaps he'll knock down the price a little, Åsgaut says

He did for me, he says

I didn't have as much as he asked, and perhaps that was a good thing, because he let me buy it for what I had, he says

and they walk along the Wharf and Olav thinks that this is a special moment, here he is, a miserable man like him, on his way to buy the finest gift for his loved one, not bad, is it, he thinks, even if he has come to Bjørgvin to buy rings, he may as well buy a bracelet, he can always buy rings later, he thinks, for now, now that he has seen the finest bracelet, in the yellowest gold and with the bluest of blue pearls, yes, now it would be difficult not to buy such a bracelet for Åsta, so that, that's what he'll do, Olav thinks, and he hears Åsgaut saying that the bracelet, yes, it's very fine, it's beautiful, they say, he says, and Olav says that yes, yes it is fine, it is such a fine bracelet that there could hardly be any finer bracelet, he says

No I don't think so, Åsgaut says

What don't you think, Olav says

That you can get a finer bracelet than this, Åsgaut says

No I don't think you can, he says

No I don't think so either, Olav says

We're almost there, Åsgaut says

But I'll follow you to the door, he says

Thank you, Olav says

I was here earlier today, and now I've come back already, he'll be wondering, that Jeweler, he says

Jeweler, Olav says

Yes, yes that's what they call him, he's called the Jeweler, Åsgaut says

That sounds fine, Olav says

Yes that's his name, Åsgaut says

Yes and he is a fine man, in all his finery, Åsgaut says

Is he now, Olav says

And he has a big black beard, yes, he says

and they keep walking along the Wharf

And you can't imagine how many fine things he has in his stall, Åsgaut says

I won't say any more about it, you can see for yourself when you get there, he says

and Olav nods and then Åsgaut takes a right turn and
walks in between two rows of houses, and the street is
quite wide between the houses and they pass door after
door and Åsgaut walks a few meters ahead of Olav and
he walks quickly, as if he's excited, and Olav hurries too,
and then Åsgaut stops in front of a large window at the
end of the alley, and there, in the window, silver and gold
are glistening and glimmering and Olav feels that he has
become quite awestruck by seeing all this splendor, it's
unbelievable that there can be so much silver and gold in
the same place, displayed in the same window

When the Jeweler isn't here, there are big shutters in
front of the windows, Åsgaut says

But now, now he seems to be here, he says

and Åsgaut walks toward a door next to the window

But over there, there's another window, Olav says

Yes there are two windows, Åsgaut says

and Olav walks over to the other window, and there, in
the middle of the window, there's a bracelet that shines in
the yellowest gold and with the bluest of blue pearls, and
it looks just like the bracelet Åsgaut has bought

There, there's the bracelet, Olav says

Yes, yes there it is, Åsgaut says

And it wasn't there when I looked in the window earlier
today, he says

The Jeweler must've put it there just now, he says

Let's go in, he says

and Olav stays there and looks and looks at all the love-
liness in that window

Let's go in, before someone else comes and buys that
fine bracelet, Åsgaut says

and he opens the door and holds the door open for
Olav and he walks in and there in front of him on the

floor stands the Jeweler himself and he bows and he says welcome, welcome to my humble selection in my humble stall, he says, still, I believe you respectable men might find something to your liking, he says, so welcome you are, welcome and what can I help you with, he says

Yes, Åsgaut says

Yes well, the Jeweler says

Yes you and I did some trade earlier today, he says

Right you are, right you are, Åsgaut says

And perhaps the gentleman wants to trade some more, the Jeweler says

No not me, but perhaps my friend here, Åsgaut says

and Olav stands and looks around, and there is such an incredible amount of silver and gold, rings and jewels and candleholders and bowls and plates and silver and gold wherever you look, just imagine that this exists in this world, so much, wherever you look, silver and gold

What can I help you with, the Jeweler says

Just imagine that so much silver and gold exists, Olav says

That it's possible, he says

Well it isn't that much, really, the Jeweler says

But a few things, yes there are a few things here, he says

And he rubs his hands together

Such an incredible amount, Olav says

And what does the gentleman desire, the Jeweler says

I, yes, I want to buy a bracelet, Olav says

Just like the one I bought earlier today, Åsgaut says

Yes then you're lucky, the Jeweler says

and he claps his hands together, several times he claps them together, as if he were applauding

Then you're lucky, because it's not easy to get hold of fine bracelets like that these days, he says

Not at all, he says

They're almost impossible to find these days, he says

and he says that he still managed to get two bracelets like that, mostly because he has many years experience, and knows so many people, that's why he could do it, he says, to tell the truth, the bracelets came in yesterday and today already he sold the first one and he nods at Åsgaut, to that gentleman there, yes, he managed to get one of the them, yes he was lucky, he says, and several others have already been here to look at the other one, so now, now this gentleman is extremely lucky, because incredibly, the other bracelet is still here, and it's even on display in the window, he says and bows and he asks the gentlemen to excuse him for a minute and he puts on a pair of white gloves and then he walks over and lifts the bracelet from the window and places it carefully down on a table

Now this is excellent craftsmanship, the Jeweler says

It's excellent craftsmanship, it's art, he says

And he strokes his forefinger carefully over the bracelet

And you want to buy this, he says

and he looks humbly at Olav

Yes, yes I can understand that, the Jeweler says

Yes well if I have enough money, Olav says

Yes, in the end that's what it always comes down to, the Jeweler says

and his voice seems full of woe and worry and Olav takes the three bills he has left from his pocket and he hands them to the Jeweler and he takes them and looks at each of the bills

That's too little, yes, he says

That's too little, Olav says

Yes it is, the Jeweler says

I can sell this for two or three more, and even that

would be a bit low, yes even that is much too cheap, he
says

and Olav feels a great despair rolling over him, because
how can he get hold of another bill, perhaps later, but not
now, and it's the finest bracelet there is in the world now,
and not later, and the Jeweler says that so many people
want to buy the bracelet

He doesn't have any more, Åsgaut says

That's all he has, the Jeweler says

And he pretends that he is appalled

But you, perhaps you can help, he says

I also gave you everything I have earlier today, Åsgaut
says

and the Jeweler shakes his head and his face looks
dismayed

Oh no, oh no, he says

Yes, I suppose we should leave then, Åsgaut says and
he looks at Olav

Yes, Olav says

and Åsgaut walks toward the door and Olav holds out
his hand to the Jeweler

Oh well then, the Jeweler says

and with a brusque movement he puts the three bills
in his pocket and his voice is a little angry

That'll have to do then, he says

and he lifts the bracelet up in the air and hands it to
Olav and then Olav stands there with the finest bracelet
in his hand, in the yellowest gold, with the bluest of blue
pearls, and he cannot believe what he's seeing, he cannot
believe that he's standing there and holding such a beautiful bracelet in his hand and he looks and he sees the
bracelet hanging around Åsta's arm, as if it were real, just

imagine such a thing, he thinks, that something like this should happen, he thinks

Come on, Åsgaut says

Yes it's really too bad, I should not have done this, it's a shame to sell such a fine bracelet for such a small sum, the Jeweler says

I make a loss on this trade, he says

and his voice is high and whining and Åsgaut is standing there holding the door open

I can't do this, the Jeweler says

I can't sell at a loss, he says

And Åsgaut is standing there holding the door open

Come on, Olav, he says

and Olav walks out the door and Åsgaut closes the door behind him and then Olav stands outside, at the end of the alley, and he looks at the bracelet he's holding in his hand, imagine that such a thing should happen, imagine that he should've found such a beautiful bracelet, Olav thinks, and he hears Åsgaut saying that they should get away from the Jeweler before he changes his mind and then Åsgaut walks down the alley and Olav walks behind him while he looks and looks at the bracelet, well imagine, he thinks, no this can't be true, he thinks, and Åsgaut says he must put the bracelet in his pocket so no one sees it and gets the idea to steal it from him, he says, and Olav puts his hand in his pocket and still holding the bracelet he walks behind Åsgaut down the alley and they come out on the Wharf again and Åsgaut says he has a few coins left, if truth be told, but that's all, and Olav says he does as well and Åsgaut says that what he means is perhaps they should get a tankard or two, because this must be celebrated, that they have both bought a bracelet each, of the finest kind, for their dear ones, Åsgaut says

    Yes of course, Olav says

    Let's drop by Skjenkjestova, Åsgaut says

    Yes, yes, we can do that, Olav says

    We'll do that then, Åsgaut says

    and they walk with steady steps up toward Skjenkjestova
and there, there up in the street, isn't that the Girl he sees,
yes so it is, the one with the long fair hair and she is walking along holding someone's arm, yes, yes so she is, just
like a short while ago she held his arm she is now holding
someone else's arm, and that's a good thing, he thinks,
good that it's someone else she's holding on to and not
him, Olav thinks, and he clasps the bracelet in his pocket

    A tankard will taste good, Åsgaut says

    Yes, Olav says

    Yes, now the girls we are engaged to have something to
look forward to, Åsgaut says

    If only they knew, Olav says

    Yes, it'll be a great pleasure to come home, Åsgaut says

    I can just see how nice the bracelet will look on Åsta's
arm, Olav says

    And I on Nilma's arm, Åsgaut says

    and they keep walking, with steady steps, and Olav
sees the Girl pulling the man whose arm she is holding
in between two houses, and it's probably the same alley
she pulled him into that she's now pulling the other man
into, he thinks

    A tankard's well deserved, Åsgaut says

    It'll taste good, he says

    Yes, Olav says, and he sees Åsgaut stop in front of the
door to Skjenkjestova, the big brown door, and Åsgaut
walks in and Olav holds the door and then he walks in

too and then they both stand there in the long hallway
with big brown logs lying on top of each other and Åsgaut
begins to walk down the hallway and then Olav follows
him and all the time he clasps the bracelet in his pocket,
and they go in, and everything is like before in there, there
at a table sits the Old Man, of course he has to be there, no
matter where he is, he is there, it's always like that, Olav
thinks, and the Old Man looks at him

So there you are, the Old Man says

I knew you'd come, I've been waiting for you, he says

I knew you'd come back to offer me a bill, he says

You wouldn't dare do otherwise, would you Asle, he
says

and the Old Man stands up and he walks toward Olav

I never doubted that you'd come back, he says

And I was right, he says

and Olav sees that Åsgaut is already at the counter holding a tankard in each hand and he walks over to Åsgaut
who holds out one of the tankards to him

It's on me, Åsgaut says

and he takes his tankard

Cheers, he says

And Olav lifts his tankard

Cheers, Olav says

and they toast and the Old Man comes over and stands
in front of them

But what about me, shouldn't I get something to drink,
huh, are you the only ones who get to have something to
drink, he says

Be clever, Asle, he says

Do as I say, he says

Buy an old man a tankard, he says

and he cocks his head a little to the side and looks up at Olav at an angle, eyes squinting

You know what I've said to you, don't you, he says

You know what I know, don't you, Asle, he says

Now stop with that begging, Åsgaut says

I'm not begging, I've never begged, I'm only asking for what is rightly mine, the Old Man says

I, I think I have to go, Olav says

But your tankard, you haven't finished your tankard, you've only just had a sip, Åsgaut says

Yes, but you can drink it, you can manage two tankards, Olav says

Yes, yes of course I can, Åsgaut says

But take another good swallow, he says

And Olav lifts the tankard to his mouth and drinks as much as he can and then he hands the tankard to Åsgaut and says he must go, he knows he must, he can't be here any longer, Olav says, and he walks toward the door

But wait, wait, the Old Man says

You promised to buy me a tankard, he says

You'd better watch out, watch out, watch out, he says

You've been warned, he says

And Olav opens the door and he walks down the long dark hallway and he walks out and then he stands in the street outside Skjenkjestova and he is wondering where he will go now, the evening is setting in and he must find somewhere to sleep, but it probably won't be in a house and that doesn't really matter, it's not all that cold, but he has to find somewhere or other to stay, he thinks, and he looks around and in a window just above him he sees an old woman standing and looking out, she has long thick gray hair and she is half hidden by a curtain, but she is probably just standing there looking and looking, Olav thinks, she's not looking for him, he thinks, and why would she be looking for him, why would he think that, what makes him think that this woman is standing there looking for him, there's no reason for him to think that, Olav thinks, and he grasps the bracelet in his pocket and he looks up and the woman is still there, half hidden by the curtain, and she's looking at him, yes, she is, he thinks, and why is the woman standing there and looking at him, what does she want, he thinks, and he looks at the window again and the woman is still standing there, she's standing there half hidden behind the curtain and then he doesn't see the woman any longer, and he can't just stand there, evening has come and he must find somewhere he can stay tonight, he thinks, he must go somewhere, he thinks, but where, where should he go, he thinks, and then he sees an old woman with long thick gray hair standing in the street over there

You, the Old Woman says

You look like you need lodgings, she says

Isn't that right, she says

and Olav doesn't quite know what to answer

Answer me now, she says

I can tell, she says

Do you, she says

and Olav says that he cannot really deny it, no, and she says that if he needs lodgings he should come with her and she'll look after him, she says, and he thinks why not and then he walks over to her and she turns and walks through the door she was standing in front of and then he watches her walk up some stairs and he follows her and he hears her puffing up the stairs and between breaths she says

that she can give him a room for the night, and it won't be
expensive, no, she says, and when she has arrived at the top
of the stairs she stops and stands there and huffs and puffs,
a bed for the night can be arranged, she says, and he stops
on the stairs and she opens a door and walks through and
he walks up and he walks in after her and he sees that there
is a girl with long fair hair looking out the window and the
Old Woman walks over to her and stands next to her, just
the way she stood before and he stands there and looks at
them and then he hears the Old Woman say that he's finally
leaving Skjenkjestova and then the question is whether he
has the sense to go home again, or if he'll keep going, but
he'll have nothing left to buy a drink with, where should he
have that from she says, and the Girl says that there isn't a
coin left in this place, so what are they going to live off of,
how are they going to get something to eat, the Girl says,
and she turns to Olav and he sees that she is the Girl he
met earlier that day, who took his arm and led him into a
narrow alley, that's the Girl, and of course it had to be her,
he thinks, and the Girl looks at him, and she seems to be
grinning a little, and now she's nodding to him

    You don't have any bills either, do you, the Girl says
    No, Olav says
    and the Old Woman turns and looks at him
    Obviously you can't get lodgings in my house if you
can't pay for yourself, she says
    I thought you knew that much, she says
    But surely you have a few coins at least, she says
    A few coins, she says
    I'm sure you're not quite penniless either, she says
    You're not that badly off, I'm sure, she says
    Or, she says

and she stands there and looks at him

And who are you, she says

Me, Olav says

I know him, the Girl says

Just so you know, she says

So you do, do you, the Old Woman says

But coins, you don't have any of them, she says

Who said that, Olav says

You've got bills, the Girl says

and she goes and puts her arms around him and the Old Woman shakes her head and then the Girl leans against him and kisses his cheek

Look at how you're behaving, the Old Woman says

and the Girl licks her way to his mouth and then she kisses him

Yes, well I suppose that was all I could expect, the Old Woman says

and then the Girl slides around him and then she stands there and pushes herself against his chest

A beautiful and poor girl in the bloom of youth, the Old Woman says

and the Girl puts both her hands on his buttocks

But still, the Old Woman says

and the Girl fondles him

Imagine me having to watch something like this, the Old Woman says

and Olav stands there with his arms straight

I'd never have thought that about you, the Old Woman says

and Olav thinks that this, what is this, he can't be here, he thinks

You, you, you, my own daughter, the Old Woman says

and the Girl licks his neck

Disgracing yourself like this, the Old Woman says

and Olav thinks that now he must leave, why is he standing there like this with the Girl, no, this isn't possible, he thinks

I'd thought I'd get you well married, but no, if this is how you are, there'll be no question of that, the Old Woman says

and Olav takes the Girl's arms and frees himself and she puts her arms around him again and strokes his back and he moves away from her

What kind of a guy are you, the Girl says

No, no, no, it seems we've been stricken with all sorts of bad luck, the Old Woman says

You're awful, the Girl says

You're the worst guy in the whole of Bjørgvin, she says

No one's worse than you, she says

No everything is awful, she says

and then the Old Woman goes and sits down in a chair with her head in her hands and he sees the Girl standing there with both fists clenched and then the Old Woman says that everything is awful, everything is awful and then the Girl says that she can't say anything else, always that, that everything is awful, everything is awful, she's always saying that, she says, and then she shakes a fist at the Old Woman and says that she's always complaining about her, always, as if she was any better when she was young, ha, oh no she wasn't, she says

Were you so much better, she says

What do you know about that, the Old Woman says and looks sharply at the Girl

What I know, I know what I know, I understand what I understand, the Girl says

And I'm right, aren't I, she says

It's not him who lives here that's my father, I know that much, she says

And have I ever said that, the Old Woman says

Yes you have, the Girl says

So I have then, the Old Woman says

It could well be him, she says

But it's not certain, the Girl says

No I suppose it's not certain, the Old Woman says

So who my father is, no you don't know that, the Girl says

I've said who I think it is, the Old Woman says

And you're yelling at me, the Girl says

and Olav stands there and hears the Old Woman say that she doesn't yell at her, she's never yelled at her, now and then she has asked her to help her with something perhaps, she says, to lend a hand, to give a coin or two when she didn't have anything for food, she's looked after her, she has, for all those years since she was born she's looked after her and it hasn't been easy, she's cost her a lot over all those years and the thanks she gets is being yelled at and called something neither of them would name and then, no this is too much for her, the Old Woman says, and she covers her face with her hands and she sobs loudly and painfully and the Girl says that if she hasn't been any better herself, she shouldn't complain about her, how silly is that, complaining about your own daughter when you haven't been any better yourself, she says, and the Old Woman says, and she almost screams it, that of course she wanted her daughter to have a better life than she herself has had and she had done her best for that to happen and then the thanks she gets is to be scolded, and by her own and only daughter too, no how can that be possible, she says, and

the Girl says what else can she do and the Old Woman
says that she doesn't believe that, there are many things
you can do, she's lived for a long while, she says, and the
Girl says tell me, tell me then, tell me what I can do and
the Old Woman says that she can do many things, she can
sew, she can sell goods in a stall, she can sell goods at the
Market Place, she can, like her sister, who disappeared so
suddenly and strangely, be a midwife, she can do whatever
she likes, she says, and the Girl says exactly, yes, exactly,
that's exactly what she's doing and the Old Woman says
that following her desires, that's not what she means by
doing what she wants, or she should follow her desires,
but not in that way, she must use her desires to get herself
a respectable life and a respectable income, she must get
married and become a decent person, she must have a husband and children, she must behave herself, she mustn't
throw herself at different men for little and nothing, yes,
yes that's what she herself did and how little did she have
left now for having done that, nothing, she had nothing
left, just the shame, because perhaps that's well and good,
in its way, as long as it lasts, but it doesn't last, you're only
just getting close to the years when you can safely do what
you like, when it's over, yes, yes over, then it's over and no
one will ever offer you anything anymore, that's how the
tune goes, she says, and the Girl says of course that's how
it is and so you have to enjoy it while you can, she says,
and the Old Woman says that she has never heard anyone
saying anything so senseless and stupid, she, she has lived
for a long time and she knows what she's talking about,
so instead of being stubborn she should listen to someone
who's lived for a long time and has experience in talking
and behaving accordingly, she says, and the Girl says that

she can't stand listening to her gabbing any longer and she
stands in front of Olav and she opens the top of her dress
and she holds her breasts up to him and the Old Woman
stands up and walks over and grabs the sleeve of her dress

No this is going too far, the Old Woman says

No look at this, she says

Offering yourself like this, she says

No, no, she says

and she grabs the Girl's hair and pulls her toward her

Ow, let go, the Girl says

Stop this, the Old Woman says

You whore, you whore, the Girl says

You say whore, the Old Woman ways

Whore, whore, the Girl says

and she grabs the Old Woman's arm and pulls it to her
mouth and she bites and the Old Woman lets go

You devil, you devil, the Old Woman says in a whiny
voice

That's the thanks I get, you devil, she says

Out, out, out of my house, she says

Out you whore, she says

and the Girl buttons up her dress

Take your things and go, the Old Woman says

Yes you do that, she says

Do it now, at once, she says

I'll come and get my things later, the Girl says

Yes you do that then, the Old Woman says

and then Olav sees the Girl walking along the hallway
and she opens the door and walks out and the Old Man
is standing there in the doorway and he just stands there
and looks at Olav and the Old Man says what on earth is
he doing here, because he's got no business in his abode,

is he an intruder too, that as well, perhaps, he says, and if
he'd bought him a tankard down there at Skjenkjestova,
yes then it would be another matter, but did he do that,
oh no, no he didn't, as soon as he'd hinted at it, he finished his drink and left and now, now he stood there in
his abode, in his lodgings and what business does he have
there, he says, and then he says that now, now he'll go and
get the Law, and then the Law will have to take care of
him, because it, the Law, has a lot to talk to Asle about, he
says, and there stands the Old Woman and she says to the
Old Man no, what's he saying, how could that be, what
wrong had Asle done, she says, and Olav walks toward the
door and the Old Man stretches out his arms and grasps
the doorframe with both hands and he stands there and
blocks the door

You go and get the Law, the Old Man says

Me, the Old Woman says

Yes you, yes, he says

But I can't get past you, she says

All right, he says

Why should I get the Law, she says

Don't ask, he says

Just do it, he says

All right if that's what you say, she says

And she walks toward Olav and when she walks past
him her long thick gray hair brushes against his arm and
then the Old Man lifts one arm and lets her out and he
looks at Olav

This is how it goes with people like you, Asle, he says

and then the Old Man comes inside and he closes the
door behind him

You were after my daughter, perhaps, the Old Man says

You were after my daughter, but that didn't work, did it, instead of getting a treat you'll get a rope around the neck in Pynten, he says

That, that's how it goes with people like you, Asle, he says

You're a killer, he says

You've killed, oh yes I know, he says

And he who kills shall himself be killed, he says

That's the Law, that's God's law, he says

and he pulls out a key and he locks the door behind him and he turns around

There, he says

and he takes a few steps toward Olav

So your name's Olav, is it, he says

and he grabs his arm

Olav, yes, he says

Your name was Olav, he says

Nothing else, only that, he says

Olav, yes, he says

Yes, Olav says

And when did you start calling yourself that, he says

It's my Christian name, Olav says

Oh yes, I see, the Old Man says

Now I think you should come with me, he says

Are you coming willingly or do I have to use force, he says

Why should I come with you, Olav says

You'll know soon, the Old Man says

I want to know before I come with you, Olav says

Now that, I decide that, the Old Man says

and he lets go of his arm

No, the Old Man says

No the best is to wait for the Law to come, till she's
fetched the Law, he says

You're young and strong and I'm old, he says

You could try and escape from me, couldn't you, he says

But now, now the Law will soon be here, he says

and he looks at Olav

Do you know what's waiting for you, he says

No, no you probably don't, he says

No you don't know that, he says

And that's just as well, he says

Yes, I should say it is, he says

and then someone pulls the door handle and the Old
Woman shouts open why don't you and then the Old
Man goes and unlocks the door and then Olav sees that
the Old Woman is standing there and behind her stands a
fellow of his own age and he is dressed in black and behind
him stands another man about the same age and he too
is dressed in black

There he is, the Old Man says

and then the two men walk over to Olav and they
put his arms behind his back and then they tie his arms
together and then they hold him, each taking an arm,
and then the men pull him along with them toward the
door and he hears the Old Man saying that this, yes this
is how he ends up, this is how Asle from Dylgja ends up,
he says, and what else could he expect, because he who
has killed shall himself be killed, as it is written, he says,
and Olav turns and he sees the Old Man standing there in
the doorway and their eyes meet and then the Old Man
says that this is how it goes with someone who doesn't buy
him a tankard, with someone who, even if he has money,
refuses to share it, he says, then you have to earn some

money another way, a reward, has Asle heard about that, no no, never, he's never heard about that, has he, no, but there is something called a reward, it exists, yes it does, he says, and then he grins and Olav turns and the two men lead him down the stairs and out onto the street and they walk quickly down the street, one man on each side of him and both have a good grip on his arms and no one says anything and he thinks that the best thing would be not to say anything and there ahead he sees the Girl and she sees him and she says well well, look at who's walking there so fine and free, she says, well it was so nice to see you again, she says, and then she lifts an arm and holds it up and there, around her arm, hangs the fine bracelet, the finest bracelet in the yellowest gold and with the bluest of blue pearls and she stands there with her arm raised and then she waves to Olav and she smiles at him, no, no, he thinks, she has stolen the bracelet, she must have put her hand in his pocket, he thinks, and that, that which should have been on Åsta's arm, now, now it glitters and glistens on the Girl's arm and she comes over to them and she begins to walk alongside them and all the time she's holding up the arm with the bracelet in front of her and her long fair hair lifts up and falls down, lifts and falls as she walks and then she says that she could almost have said that she was longing to see him again, she says, but now, he's not much good now, she says, and all the time she's holding up her arm with the bracelet toward him, there's not much about him anymore, she says, but when he's released again, yes then he must come, then he can come back to her again, she says, and then she holds up her arm with the brace-let right in front of his eyes and then she says look, look isn't it nice, imagine you giving me such a nice bracelet, she says, but thank you, thank you so much, she says, I'll always be grateful to you for it, she says, and then she says that once he has been released, he'll be given something in return for the bracelet, she can promise him that, so thank you thank you for the bracelet, she says, and he closes his eyes and he lets the two men lead him wherever they want and they walk along the street and then he hears the Girl calling thank you, thank you for the bracelet, yes, as I said, she calls, and he doesn't want to open his eyes and he walks steadily forward and where is Åsta, where is little Sigvald, where are Åsta and little Sigvald, Olav thinks, and he walks along steadily, quite steadily, with his eyes closed and then he sees Åsta standing there in front of him holding little Sigvald to her breast, you're standing there outside the house in Barmen, my good Åsta, my best, he thinks and then he hears himself say that perhaps it's best if from then on they say that his name is Olav and not Asle, he says, and Alida asks why and he just says he thinks it would be best, safest, if someone wanted to find them for some reason or other, he says, and she asks why would anyone want to find them and he says he doesn't know, but he believes that it's probably best if they change names and then she yes if that's what he thinks, yes that's how it must be, she says

So now I'm Olav, not Asle, he says

And I'm Åsta and not Alida, she says

and then he says that now Olav is walking into the house and she says that Åsta is walking into the house with him, and he opens the door and they walk in

But little Sigvald, he can still be Sigvald, she says

Yes of course, Åsta, he says

Oh Olav, Olav, she says

and then she laughs

Asta, Åsta, he says and he laughs too

And our last name is Vik, he says

Åsta and Olav Vik, he says

Olav and Åsta and then little Sigvald, she says

That's how it is now, he says

But how long do you think we can live here, she says

For quite a long time, he says

But someone must own the house, she says

Yes, yes there must be someone, but perhaps they're dead, he says

Do you think so, she says

It was empty when we arrived here, and it's probably been empty for some time, he says

But still, she says

It's a fine place to live, she says

It's good to live here, he says

Yes, she says

And there's still a lot of the cured leg of ham left, he says

Yes, she says

Yes I was lucky to find it, he says

Find it, she says

They had more than enough on that farm, he says

But you shouldn't steal from neighbors, she says

If you must, you must, he says

Perhaps that's how it is, she says

And I'll catch fish, he says

But that boat, don't you think, she says and breaks off

The boat's lying there well moored, he says

Yes we'll manage, she says

You and I will manage, he says

You and I and little Sigvald, she says

Åsta and Olav Vik, she says

Everything's going well, he says

and then he says he must take a trip to Bjørgvin one of these days, he has an errand to do there

Must you, she says

No but I have something I want to buy there, he says

Perhaps you shouldn't have sold the fiddle, she says

Because I sold the fiddle, I can now buy something in Bjørgvin, he says

But, he says

Yes, she says

Then we must have something to eat on that day, too, he says

Yes, on most days, she says

Yes, that you must, he says

and then Olav says that perhaps he should go into Bjørgvin today, he's been thinking about it for a while and today's the day, he says, and Åsta says that no, not today, because then she'll be alone in Barmen and that's not very nice to think about, so many things can happen, so many kinds of people can come by, she doesn't like to be alone, she says, everything's so much nicer when there's the two of them, she says, and Olav says that he'll come back as soon as he can, he'll hurry, he'll walk as fast as he can and then he'll buy what he's thinking of buying and then he'll come back to her with the thing he's bought, yes he won't be away for too long, he says, and she says that perhaps she and little Sigvald can come with him and he says of course they can, there's nothing he'd rather, but it'll be faster if he goes alone, he says, if they both go, and have to carry little Sigvald, it will take so long to get to Bjørgvin, but if he walks alone it doesn't have to take all that long, he'll hurry, as fast as he can, he'll hurry so that he'll be back quickly to her and little Sigvald, he says, and Åsta says she supposes what he says is true, but then he must promise her to not even look at the girls there in Bjørgvin, she says, and he must never start chatting with them, for those girls have only one thing on their mind and one thing only and they are so barefaced there, they walk around, horny and gossiping about all the others, he must promise, he mustn't talk to them, she says, and Olav says that it isn't to talk to the girls that he's going to Bjørgvin, and she says yes well, she knows that, but still, it's not what he wants that worries her, no not at all, it's the girls there, and their determination and their power that worry her, because the girls in Bjørgvin know what they want, they are not to be trifled with, she says, and then she says that he mustn't go, he cannot go, she can see him with another girl, and it's a nice girl, a girl with long fair hair, oh how awful, she says, oh such a fair and foul girl, such fair hair, and with such blue eyes, not black-haired like her, not with brown eyes like her, oh how awful, Åsta says, and she says that no, he can't go to Bjørgvin today, something bad will happen to them then, something bad will happen, something awful, something terribly awful, something she doesn't even dare to think about will happen then, something unbearable, something that will destroy everything, he'll disappear, just like Pa Aslak disappeared he too will disappear, disappear forever, she can feel it, she knows it, and she is so certain, she knows it for certain, she must tell him, she can't not tell him, it must be said, she says, and then she takes his hand and she grabs his hand and she says that he mustn't leave her, for then she will never see him again, she says, and he says that no, he must go to Bjørgvin today, it's a long walk, and today the weather's good, there's no wind, there's no rain, she can see for herself how the fjord lies there glittering and calm, how blue the fjord is today, and it's mild, today's the day to go to Bjørgvin, he's sure of that, and if someone should come and ask his name, or ask her name, she must say that his name's Olav and her name's Åsta, the way they've decided, and should someone ask where they come from, she doesn't have to blurt out that they come from Dylgja, he says, and she asks where she should say they come from and he says they come from some place outside Bjørgvin, further north, called Vik, because there must be places north of Bjørgvin called Vik, he says, and she says all right then, she's from Vik, her name's Åsta and comes from Vik and so her full name is Åsta Vik then and he says yes, yes that it is, and his full name is Olav Vik. Now this is what they're called from now on. Now they're called Åsta and Olav Vik, they're married, and they have a son, Sigvald. They were married in the church in Vik and their son Sigvald was christened there later and they haven't got around to buying rings yet, but they'll do that very soon, she must say that, he says

All right then Olav Vik, she says

That's what we'll say Åsta Vik, he says

and they smile at each other and now, he says, now he, Olav Vik, will go to Bjørgvin, because he has an errand to do there and when the errand is done he will come straight home to her and to little Sigvald, he says

Yes, you must do that, she says

I must, he says

and then Åsta sees him standing there in the doorway and he smiles at her and then he quickly closes the door and then she is alone again, she and little Sigvald, and she

can feel it, she feels it with her whole self, that she will
never see Olav again, and he mustn't go, he mustn't go to
Bjørgvin today, she thinks, but she has already told him,
she has told him what she knows, but he won't listen to
her, she can say whatever she wants, but he still won't listen
to what she's saying, and she won't go out, she won't watch
him walking away from her, she won't see him again for
the last time, because now she has seen her man, her love,
for the last time, she thinks, and from now on she is called
Åsta, and he is called Olav, and she has seen her Olav for
the last time now, what happened to Pa Aslak would happen to him, he too walked away and was gone forever, and
now she was on her own again, she and little Sigvald are
now just the two of them, and that's what they'll be, from
now on there's just the two of them left, Åsta thinks, and
then little Sigvald begins to cry and she lifts him up and
she rocks him, she holds him against her breast and she
rocks him and he cries and cries and she rocks him and
says don't cry, don't cry my good little boy, she says, and
she rocks him, don't cry, my good little boy, don't cry, she
says, don't cry, don't weep in the hay don't sleep, she says,
don't laugh, don't whine don't sit and pine, this house is
yours and mine, in this house Ma Alida and little Sigvald
will live, here they will live, here they will stay, here they
will toil and till the soil, Ma Alida will weave and Sigvald
will float across the sea in his boat, so don't cry, everything
will be fine and one day a castle will come, one day the
castle will come, she says, and little Sigvald stops crying
and Olav makes a leap and the men who hold onto his
arms leap too and then they say what is he trying to do,
does he think it's that easy to get away from them, no now
he should just take it easy, soon he won't wriggle around at

all, soon he'll lie there dead and immovable the way someone who has killed others deserves to lie, killing shall be
paid with killing, he won't be wriggling around very much
longer, oh no, the Hangman will see to that, he knows
that business, the Hangman, he's an expert in stopping
men like him kicking about, they say, and that's for sure,
so he may as well calm down at once, he's going out to
Pynten and many people will gather around him, almost
everyone who lives in the city of Bjørgvin will gather to see
him hanging there, the whole population of Bjørgvin will
watch him hanging there, and when he's dead and can't
move anymore they will watch him hanging there and
then they will watch him lying there dead and stiff on the
ground with a broken neck, yes they will, so he may as well
stop that kicking about, he can always kick and wriggle his
arms and legs around when the Hangman hangs him, he
can leap and wriggle as much as he likes then, but till then
he can save himself all the leaping and wriggling, they tell
him and then pull him hard and they continue along and
he can't quite keep up with them and he sinks down on
his knees and they pull him on his knees along the street
and it hurts and he manages to get back on his feet again
and then they are once more walking steadily forward and
then they say that they'll soon be there and they say yes
they are, and that's a good thing, so they don't have to haul
along this lazy lout any longer, then they'll be rid of him,
once they get him into the Pit and close the door properly
behind them, that's their work done, and then others will
have to take over, they say, and the Hangman should be
ready in just a few days, and then justice will be done, in
everyone's presence, in front of everyone in Bjørgvin, out
there on Pynten, justice will be done, that's what they are

helping to happen, justice will be done, there must always be justice, only when the Hangman has done his work has justice been done, they say, and they turn suddenly to the right and they say that now he is going into the Pit and they say that it was certainly a good thing that he was finally caught, and all thanks to that old tramp, he'll have more to do as a hangman now, they say, and then they take a sudden right turn again and they walk down a steep staircase and Olav looks up and he looks straight into wet black rock and they pull him down the stairs and when they have come down and it is so dark that he can hardly see anything, just something gray and black which is probably a door there in front of him, they stop, and then they stand quite still. And the man in front of Olav lets go. And then he hears a rattling sound and he sees the man in front of him bend toward the door and he fumbles and swears and he gets the key into the lock and then he manages to push the door open

Not so easy when it's as dark as it is in here, he says

But I finally got it, he says

Yes, damn it, I did, he says

and the man in front of Olav walks through the door and the man behind him pulls his arm and Olav manages to put down his foot on the first step and then on the next and then he walks through the door

This is where you'll live now, the time you have left, one of them says

The time you have left, you'll spend here, the other one says

And that serves you right, he says

People like you shouldn't live, he says

Killers like you shall be killed, the other one says

And Olav stands there and then the two men walk
out and then they close the door in front of him and he
hears the sound of rattling keys and he hears the door
being locked and then he stands there and he puts both
hands against the door and then he just stands there and
he doesn't think anything, everything is empty and neither
joy nor grief can reach him and then he moves one hand
away from the door and onto a stone and the stone is wet
and he lets his hand slide slowly along the stone and he lets
his other hand slide along the stone too and then something touches one of his calves and he puts his hand down
and it seems to be a bench and then he gropes his way forward and he sits down carefully and he feels around and he
lies down and then he lies there on the bench and he looks
into the empty darkness, and he is empty, as empty as the
emptiest darkness, and he's lying there, just lying there, he
lies there and he closes his eyes and then he feels Alida's
hand there on his shoulder and he turns and he puts his
arm around her and pulls her close to him and he hears her
even breathing and she seems to be lying there asleep and
her breath is even and her body is warm and he reaches
out his hand and he feels that there next to her lies little
Sigvald and he hears that he too is breathing evenly and he
puts his hand on Alida's stomach and he lies there very still
and he doesn't move and he listens to her even breathing
and he turns and he feels that he is cold, and he is warm,
he is cold and he is warm, he is cold and he is sweating,
and Alida, where is Alida, and little Sigvald, where is little
Sigvald, and it is dark, and everything is wet, he is sweating, and is he asleep or is he awake, and why is he here,
why must he be here, why is he here in the Pit, and the
door is locked, and Alida, will he ever see Alida again, and

little Sigvald, will he ever see little Sigvald again, and why is he here in the Pit, and he is so warm, and he is so cold, and he is asleep, perhaps, he is waking up, perhaps, he is warm, he is cold, he opens his eyes and there is a slot in the door and a little light comes in and he sees the door and he sees the large rocks, rock upon rock, and he stands up, he walks over to the door and he pulls the handle, and the door is locked and he puts all his weight against the door and the door is locked and where is Alida, where is little Sigvald, he is cold, he is sweating and he looks out of the slot and can only see the rocks on the stairs, and has he been here for a long time, or has he just arrived here, will he stay here for a long time, or will he soon be let out into the light of day, will he soon walk through the streets and get back home to Alida and to little Sigvald, Alida and little Sigvald, and he, Asle, the three of them, he thinks, but his name isn't Asle anymore, his name's Olav, and even that he cannot remember, his name is Olav, Alida's name is Åsta and little Sigvald, his name is Sigvald and he starts because he hears steps and then he hears a key in the lock and he goes and sits down on the bench and surely it isn't the Hangman who has come to fetch him, that can't be how it is, no he'll get back to Åsta and to little Sigvald, yes, so no one can put a rope around his neck and string him up, of course not, they can think what they want, but that's not what's going to happen, Olav thinks, and he lies down on the bench and he stares ahead and then he sees that the door opens and a man comes into the Pit, he isn't very big, he is hunched over, stooped, and he has a gray knit cap on his head and he just stands and looks at Olav and he sees that it's the Old Man

So there's the killer, he says

with a thin and whining voice

But now justice will soon be done, Asle, he says

He who kills shall be killed, he says

and then the Old Man squints at him and he pulls out what looks like a black sack and he pulls it over his head, and he stands there in the doorway for a long time, and then he pulls the sack off his head

Did you see that, Asle, he says

with squinting eyes

I thought you should know who I am, who the Hangman is, he says

I thought you deserved to know that much, he says

Or what do you think, Asle, he says

Don't you agree, he says

Oh yes I'm sure you do, he says

I can't see why you shouldn't, he says

and then the Old Man turns and Olav hears him say that they can come now, and then the two men who took him here to the Pit enter and they stand there, one on each side of the Old Man, and a little behind him

The day and the hour has come, the Old Man says

Now I am here, he says

Now the Hangman has arrived, he says

and then he shouts to hold him and the two men walk into the Pit and they take a shoulder each and then they sit him up on the bench

Stand up, the Old Man says

and Olav stands up and they each grab an arm and they put his arms behind his back and they tie his hands together

Now walk, the Old Man shouts

and Olav takes a step forward

Walk, he shouts again

and the two men grab Olav again

Now justice shall be done, the Old Man says

and then the men begin to walk toward the door with Olav between them, each clutching an arm, and then they have come outside and they begin to walk up the stairs and when they have come to the top they stop and then Olav sees that the Old Man closes the door to the Pit and then he too comes up the stairs and he stands in front of them and he looks at Olav

Now the Law shall do its justice, the Old Man says

Now the time for justice has arrived, he says

Take him to Pynten, he shouts

Walk, he shouts

and then the Old Man begins to walk with long even steps along the street and he waves the black sack and the two men pull Olav's arms and he's walking along the street, between the two men and behind the Old Man, and then they shout the Hangman, the Hangman is here, now justice shall be done, now the dead will get their amends, now the dead will get their justice, they shout and Olav reaches out his fingers and there's no one there, he feels no one, where are you, where are you now Alida, he thinks and he reaches out his fingers a little further and there's no little Sigvald there and where are they, where are Alida and little Sigvald, he thinks, and he sees that the Old Man is waving the black sack and shouting come, come now, come and see justice being done, he shouts, now justice shall be done, now you must come, he shouts, and Olav sees that people are beginning to gather around the Old Man and around himself

Come, come, the Old Man shouts

Now justice shall happen, he shouts

Keep walking, he shouts

Now justice shall happen on Pynten, he shouts

Come, everyone come now, he shouts

Keep walking, he shouts

and Olav sees that there are many people gathered already, he is part of a whole group of followers and then he hears Alida saying aren't you going to wake up soon and he sees that she's standing on the floor only half dressed and he sits up and there on the floor he sees little Sigvald crawling around and he is almost totally naked and he hears the Old Man shouting come, come now and Olav feels that he is cold, and he is warm, and everything is empty and he closes his eyes and just walks forward and he hears screaming and yelling and nothing exists any longer, all that exists now is the soaring, no joy, no grief, now there is only the soaring left, the soaring he is, the soaring Alida is, he thinks

I am Asle, he calls

and he walks with his eyes closed

You're Asle, yes, the Old Man says

Isn't that what I've been saying all this time, he says

But you, you pretended you weren't Asle anymore, he says

You liar, he says

and Asle tries to be what he knows he is, a soaring, and the soaring is called Alida, and he just wants to glide, Asle thinks, and he hears cries and screams and then they stop

We've arrived at Pynten, the Old Man says

and Asle opens his eyes and there, in front of him, there stands Alida and against her breasts she's holding little Sigvald and she rocks him, from side to side, you just

sleep, don't you weep, just live and breathe, just be happy
and true, just live and be you, Alida says, and she rocks
little Sigvald from side to side and Asle sees the fjord so
glitteringly blue, today the fjord is blue and glittering, he
thinks, and the fjord is totally calm, he thinks, and there,
behind Alida, there is Åsgaut from Vika and he waves at
Asle and asks if his name is Asle or Olav and if he is from
Dylgja or from Vik and then there is only screaming and
shouting and then he sees the Girl come running and she
walks over to Alida and she holds her arm with the bracelet up to Alida and then the Girl looks at Asle and she
lifts her arm with the bracelet in the air and waves to him
and behind the Girl, where she stands and waves with the
bracelet, Asle sees the Jeweler come walking, slowly, slowly,
in all his finery, he comes walking toward Asle and just
behind the Jeweler the Old Woman comes walking and
she is grinning behind her long thick gray hair and her hair
comes closer and closer and all he can see is her long thick
gray hair and he sees many faces, infinitely many faces, but
there's no one he knows, and what's become of Alida, and
what's become of little Sigvald, they were there then, he
saw them, but where are they now, where are they, Asle
thinks, and then a black sack is pulled over his head and
then a rope is put around his neck and he hears screams
and cries and he feels the rope against his neck and then
he hears Alida saying there you are, you're my good boy,
you're the best boy in the world, you are there, and I am
here, there is glimmer, there is glitter, there's no fear, my
boy, my dear, and Asle is soaring along the blue glittering fjord and Alida says you must sleep my dear boy, you
must soar, live in awe, you must play, my dear boy, and
then there's a soaring along the blue glittering fjord and up

into the blue sky, and Alida takes Asle's hand and then he
stands up and then he stands there and holds Alida's hand

Weariness

ALES PULLS THE wool blanket tighter around herself, for it's a little cold, yes it is, she thinks, as she sits there in her chair and looks at the window almost completely covered by thin white curtains, the light comes in only through a tiny crack at the very bottom, she sees without seeing in a way, and then she sees someone walk past outside the window, and who it is she cannot see, but that someone walked past, that she could see, and this is where she lives, she thinks, in a small house as close to the road as you could possibly get, it turned out that she would live her life in such a house, she thinks, and if it weren't for the curtains everyone could see her where she was sitting, they could still see her sitting there now, but not clearly, they can just see that someone is sitting there, she thinks, but does it matter if someone can see her sitting there? no not at all, she thinks, it doesn't matter one little bit, she thinks, no it doesn't, she thinks, and she tries to pull the wool blanket even closer around her body and then she thinks you are Ales, yes you are old Ales, yes, she thinks, for now you've grown old, Ales, she thinks, and now you sit there in your chair and try to keep warm, she thinks, and then she thinks that she must try to stand up and put some more wood in the stove and she gets on her feet and she walks toward the stove and she opens the door to the stove and puts some more wood in the stove before she walks back to her chair, sits down, spreads the wool blanket over herself, covers herself with it and then sits there and looks straight ahead, she looks at the window in her living room but without seeing, and then she sees Alida, her mother, as she sits in her living room in Vika just like Ales now sits in her living room and now she sees Alida stand up, slowly and stiffly, and walk, with short steps, across the floor, but where is she going? Where is she headed? Is she going out? Over to the stove there in the corner? And Ales stands up and walks with short stiff steps across the floor and then Ales sees Alida open the door to her kitchen and Alida goes into her kitchen and Ales goes into hers

I'm getting old too, Ales says

The years have passed so quickly, she says

And I never saw Alida as an old woman, not alive, but now I see her so often, she says

I don't understand it, she says

I've grown old now, she says

Old, yes, she says

Mustn't talk, she says

And usually I'm just pottering around here, but they look in, now and then, one of the kids, one of the grand-kids perhaps, she says

But usually I potter around, taking short steps and talking to myself yes, she says

and Ales sees Alida sit down on the chair there by her kitchen table and Ales goes and sits down on the chair by her kitchen table, her good kitchen, Ales thinks, it's coziest here in the kitchen, she thinks, she's always thinking that, she thinks it too often, always, she's always thinking that the kitchen is the coziest room in the house, Ales thinks, her kitchen is not very big, but it's cozy, it's always been cozy, she thinks, and she has table and chairs, cupboards and a stove, just like her mother did, in one corner of her kitchen was the black stove she would light the fire in, for heat, and for cooking, and she has a stove quite like the one her mother had, and then the table in the middle of the floor, the bench along the wall, then there was the living room and the loft in the living room, the loft she remembers so well, there they slept, she and Little Sister, but that, that's so long ago, something that doesn't exist, something that has never really existed even if it has and Little Sister lying there so pale and gone and never will her pale face, her open mouth, her half-open eyes, disappear for her, she will always see it, because Little Sister became ill and died and everything went so fast, she was alive and happy and then she was ill and died, and then their big brother, Sigvald, half-brother, really, who went away when she was still only a little girl and never came back, and no one knew what had become of him, but he played the fiddle, yes, and no one had heard anyone play the fiddle as well as their half-brother Sigvald, yes he could play, and that's just about the only thing she remembers about him, and his father played the fiddle too, the one they talked about, Asle was his name and they hanged him in Bjørgvin they said, imagine hanging people the way they did in those days, in the olden days, that they could do that, that they were like that, she thinks, and her mother who got married again to her father, Åsleik, yes, yes that's how that was, that's how the story went, and her father, whose name was Åsleik and who they called Viken, because it was he who owned the place there in Vika, the little house, the barn, the boathouse, the wharf, the boat, he owned everything, all that he'd managed to get hold of, he was an enterprising man, and then Alida came there as a house servant, and she had her son Sigvald with her, the son she had with Asle, the fiddler who had been hanged, that was how that was, she came there after Asle had been hanged, at least that's what they said, but her mother had never said anything about it herself, she'd never wanted to say anything about Asle and what happened, Ales thinks, she dropped a hint now and then, she didn't ask but just hinted and then her mother went silent and walked away from her, she can't remember her mother mentioning the name Asle a single time, it was other people who told her about him, and they did so as often as they could, it was as if everyone really wanted to tell her what kind of man her mother had been with, and what was true and not true of what they told her was difficult to tell, of course, for they talked about Asle in Dylgja, that he was a fiddler, like his father before him, that he had taken her mother by brute force and gotten her pregnant, although she was only a child herself, and that he had taken her with him after first having taken the life of her mother, that is, her own grandmother, that's what they said, but if that were true, no nobody knew, and no it couldn't be like that, it was probably just the sort of thing people made up and talked about, Ales thought, and then, they said, the gossipers said, he strangled a person of his own age so he could steal his boat, that was supposed to have happened at the boathouse where his father had lived, in Dylgja, and then, in Bjørgvin, he's supposed to have strangled several others before he was caught and hanged, that's what they said, but it couldn't be true, her mother, Alida, could never have been with a man like that, a brute like that, never in this world, that wasn't possible, she knew her mother Alida

that well, she could never live with a murderer like that,
Ales thinks, and do people like that exist, murderers like
that, it was only proper that there were gallows, people
said, and there should still be gallows, at least one in each
village, they said, and what was true and not true and what
Asle had done and not done, no that she didn't know, but
he couldn't have been a murderer, he was the father, wasn't
he, of her oldest brother, her half-brother, Sigvald, Ales
thinks, he couldn't have killed her grandmother, because
they said that she was found dead in her bed in the morning and she might just as well have died the way people
usually die, she could just as well have passed away, calmly
and silently, and had a good and quite ordinary death, of
course, that's what it must have been like, Ales thinks, and
she thinks that she can't just sit here, there's almost always
something that needs doing, something or other, she
thinks, and she looks at the window there in the kitchen
and she sees Alida standing there, in the middle of the
floor, in front of the window, she's standing there so clearly,
as if she could put a hand on her shoulder, and will she try
to do that, Ales thinks, no, no she can't do that, can she,
she can't put her hand on her own long-dead mother, Ales
thinks, no she's become an old fool, she thinks, no longer
sound of mind, antisocial, but old Alida is standing there,
curse her, confound her, Ales thinks, and should she dare
to say something to her, she has so often thought about
asking her mother if what they're saying is true, that she
went into the sea, she doesn't believe it, but they do say it,
that she did, and she was found on the foreshore, they say,
but can she sit here and talk to someone who is long dead,
no she hasn't gone that mad, has she, no matter what they
think and say about her, what these young kids of hers

think and say about her, oh yes she knows what they say about her to each other and perhaps to others as well, that she's gotten too old to live alone, that's what they say, but then none of them wants to have her living with them either, at least none of them has told her that they want to, and they have enough on their hands with their own affairs, but she's still standing there, Alida is, she thinks, of course they do, more than enough with their own, they shouldn't have to worry about her as well, and why on earth should her mother, Alida, be standing there in front of the window, in front of the window in her kitchen, Ales thinks, and if her mother is going to stay in the kitchen, she'll have to go straight into the living room, Ales thinks, because she can't stay in the same room as her long-dead mother, Ales thinks, and she sees Alida turning around and looking straight at her and Alida thinks that now her little girl, her good little girl, her dear, dear little baby has become old too, that the years should pass by so fast for her too, so frighteningly fast, she thinks, but children, yes, she has her own children, too, Ales has, six of them, and they are all grown up and have made lives for themselves, they have, each and every one of them, the girls and the boys, so her daughter Ales has had a good life, Alida thinks, and she sees little Ales climb up the ladder to the loft in the living room in Vika and then she stops on the top step and she looks back at her and then she says sleep well now, mum, and Alida says you sleep well too my good girl, you're the best girl in the whole wide world, says Alida, and then Ales climbs up and disappears into the darkness in the loft, under the bedspread, there in the corner. And then Alida stands there. And then Alida walks into the living room and she goes and stands in the doorway, and she sees Åsleik

standing there down by the boat, he's not very big and he's
not very strong but his hair is thick, and his beard is big,
and his beard is still black, even if both hair and beard have
a few strands of gray here and there, just like her own black
hair, Alida thinks, and she watches him standing there,
Åsleik, looking at his boat, he's probably standing there
pondering something, Alida thinks, he's been good to her,
Åsleik, she thinks, what would've happened to her and
little Sigvald if they hadn't met Åsleik, when they were
there on the Wharf in Bjørgvin, worn-out and miserable,
she sitting against a shack, as hungry and tired as it was
possible to be, they were sitting there, but then Åsleik was
there, suddenly he was standing there, he stood there
above her and looked down on her
    No is it you Alida, Åsleik said
    and Alida looked up
    Don't you remember me, he said
    and Alida tried to think who it could be
    Åsleik, he said
    I'm Åsleik, the man who lives in Vika, he said
    In Vika at Dylgja, she said
    Yes, he said
    and then he just stood there without saying anything
    We didn't meet very often, I'm much older than you,
but I remember you from when you were a girl, he says
    I was a man, you were a girl, he says
    Don't you remember me, he says
    Yes, yes I do, Alida says
    and of course she remembers Åsleik, but only as one of
the men who stood there and talked, and she remembers
that he lived in Vika, he and his mother, but not much
more than that, she thinks, because he was older than

her, perhaps twenty-five years older, something like that, perhaps more, so you'd have to consider him among the grown-ups, she thinks

But why are you sitting here, Åsleik says

You have to sit somewhere, Alida says

Don't you have anywhere to live, Åsleik says

No, she says

You live on the street, he says

Well you have to, when you don't have a home, Alida says

You and your boy, he says

Yes we have to, she says

And you're so thin, don't you have any food to eat either, he says

No, she says

I haven't eaten today, she says

Well stand up, come, come with me, he says

and Åsleik puts his hand under her arm and helps her to her feet and then Alida stands there with little Sigvald in her arms and down at her feet are the two bundles she lugs along with her and Åsleik asks if they belong to her and she says yes and he lifts them up and then he says come and then they walk along the Wharf in Bjørgvin, Åsleik from Vika and Alida with little Sigvald on her arm walk together along the Wharf in Bjørgvin and none of them says anything and then Åsleik turns up an alley and Alida follows him and she sees his short legs taking long steps and she sees the flaps of his black jacket hanging open and she sees his black cap pulled down on his neck and he carries her two bundles in his hands and then Åsleik stops and he looks at her and he nods his head toward an alley and then he begins to walk up the alley and Alida follows

him and she holds little Sigvald against her breast and he
sleeps his soundest sleep and then Åsleik opens a door and
holds it open and Alida walks in and she looks down and
then she looks up and she sees a long narrow room with
many tables and then she notices the smell of smoked meat
and roasted ham and it smells so good that she suddenly
feels her legs giving way beneath her, but she clasps little
Sigvald tightly to her breast and pulls herself together, yes
pulls herself together, and then she stands there steady, but
she can't remember ever smelling anything so good before,
Alida thinks, and why does Åsleik bring her here, as if she
had money to buy food, she doesn't have a single coin,
Alida thinks, and she sees people sitting there eating, and
she has never smelled such a good smell of smoked meat
and roasted ham and peas before and Alida has never felt
so hungry before and never wanted food so much before,
not that she can remember, but she, well does she have
anything to buy food with, no nothing, not a single coin
does she have, and tears fill her eyes and she begins to cry,
standing there with her long black hair, and with little
Sigvald against her breast
   But why are you crying, Åsleik says
   and she doesn't answer
   No it's nothing, he says
   Come now and let's sit down, Åsleik says
   and he lifts his hand and points to the bench at the
nearest table and Alida goes over there and she sits down
and she feels that it's also warm in there, nice and warm,
and then this wonderfully good smell of smoked meat and
roasted ham and peas, yes she can smell the boiled peas as
well, and if only she had something to spend, she would
buy and eat and eat, Alida thinks, and she sees Åsleik walk

over to a counter and she looks at his back, the long black
jacket, the black cap pulled far down his neck, and now
she remembers him from Dylgja, she does when she thinks
about it, but she only just barely remembers him, he's so
much older than her, a grown man, but she remembers
him and a few men standing there together, hands in their
pockets, that's what she can remember, him standing there
talking with some other men, everyone with the same kind
of cap and with their hands in their trouser pockets, all of
them like that, Alida thinks, and she watches Åsleik turn
and then he comes walking toward her with two plates full
of smoked meat and roasted ham and peas and potatoes
and rutabaga and dumplings, for look there's dumplings
on the plates as well, just look at that, Alida thinks, who'd
have thought she'd ever see a day like this, and she sees that
both Åsleik's mouth and his big blue eyes are grinning,
the whole of him is one big grin, the whole man, and the
plates glisten and steam and Åsleik's whole face beams
when he puts a plate down in front of Alida and he puts
a knife and fork down in front of the plate and then he
says that now they'll both have something good to eat, he's
hungry at least, and she looks downright famished, Åsleik
says, and he puts the other plate down on the other side of
the table and puts down knife and fork next to the plate
and Alida puts down little Sigvald on her lap

   Yes now a proper meal of meat of roasted meat and ham
will taste good, Åsleik says

   It certainly will, he says

   And some dumplings, he says

   Long time since I had them, he says

   You get the best food in the world here in Matstova,
he says

But you've got to have something to drink, he says

Food alone isn't enough, he says

and Alida can't wait, as hungry as she now is, she can't just sit there and look at all the good food there in front of her and she cuts herself a good piece of the smoked meat and she puts it into her mouth, and my oh my what a taste, it feels as if her eyes were about to burst, that's how good it tastes, and then she must have a bite of a dumpling too, Alida thinks, and she cuts herself a big piece and she dips it in fat and she gets a bit of roasted ham on her fork too and she gets it into her mouth and a bit of fat runs down her chin and what does that matter, Alida thinks, and she breathes deeply in and out, because she has never before tasted anything as good as this, she's certain about that, Alida thinks and she chews and she tastes and she cuts herself yet another big piece of ham and puts it in her mouth with her fingers and she chews and she breathes in and she breathes out and she sees Åsleik come with a tankard of frothy beer he puts down in front of her and then he sets a tankard next to his own plate and he lifts his tankard up to her and says skål and Alida lifts her tankard, but it's so heavy and she is so weak that she can hardly manage to lift it, but she does manage, and she holds the tankard up to Åsleik and she says skål and then she sees Åsleik lift the tankard to his mouth and take a big swallow and beer is frothing over his beard and Alida lifts her tankard to her mouth and she sips the beer, for to be honest, she never liked beer that much, it's usually sour and bitter, but this beer, yes it is sugary and light and mild, even sweetish, Alida thinks, and she has another taste of the beer and she thinks that yes, yes this is good beer, Alida thinks, and she sees Åsleik sitting down and he cuts himself a big piece of roasted ham and he puts it in his mouth and then he sits there and chews

First-rate, Åsleik says

They certainly know how to make a good meal at Matstova, he says

That was well-smoked and well-salted meat, yes, he says

Ha, what do you say, he says

The best I've ever tasted, Alida says

Yes, I'll almost say the same, Åsleik says

And the dumplings, they were good too, he says

Yes, Alida says

Yes the best I've tasted, she says

and she sees Åsleik cut a good piece of a dumpling and he gets the piece into his mouth and he chews and chews and in between chewing he says first-rate, these were first-rate dumplings, they can certainly make a good meal at Matstova, you can't make better dumplings, you can't buy better dumplings anywhere, he says and Alida takes a bite of the rutabaga, for there's rutabaga there, too, and tastes the peas, and everything tastes just as excellent, never before has anything she has eaten tasted so good, if anything it had to be the salted and dried ribs of mutton at Ma Silja's place on Christmas Eve, Alida thinks, but no, no that didn't taste as good either, this smoked meat, these soft dumplings, this, all of it, must be the best things she has tasted in her whole life, Alida thinks, and Åsleik says that yes, this tastes good and he shoves a piece of dumpling into the fried fat and the fried ham and he chews and eats dumplings shoved into the fat with fried pieces of ham in it

My god was I hungry, he says

Yes this was proper food, he says

and Alida eats and she sighs and she feels that the worst
hunger is over, and now it just tastes good, though not as
good as the first bites, of course, but she has nothing to pay
with, so how can she just sit here and eat the best food in
Bjørgvin if she can't pay for herself, no what a mess she's
making of it, Alida thinks, oh no, no what's she done, but
it tastes so good, no oh no, she thinks, no what a mess she
has made of it, Alida thinks, no she mustn't eat any more,
she mustn't, and the worst hunger has been sated, and she
hadn't eaten in many days, just drank water, and then to
be given this to eat, she can't believe it, Alida thinks, and
now, now she must get out of here somehow, as quietly as
possible, she thinks, but how can she manage that, Alida
thinks, and Åsleik looks up at her
   Didn't the food taste good, he says
   and he looks at her with big blue eyes that don't understand and are a little confused Yes, yes, Alida says
   But, she says
   Yes, Åsleik says
   and Alida doesn't say anything
   What is it, he says
   I, she says
   Yes, he says
   I don't have anything to pay with, she says
   and Åsleik lifts up his arms so that fat flies off the knife
and fork and he looks at Alida with happy open blue eyes
   But I do, he says
   and he slams his fist in the table so that the plates lift
from the tabletop and the tankards make a little jump too
there on the table and all eyes turn toward them
   Yes I do, Åsleik says
   and smiles broadly

This man has money in his pocket, he says, oh yes he does, he says

And how can you possibly think that I wouldn't treat you to a meal, he says

What would it look like if I didn't treat a hungry, yes, starving, fellow villager to a meal, he says

What kind of man would that make me, he says

Oh no, I'm paying, he says

and Alida says thank you, thank you so much, but that's far too much, she says

and Åsleik says that it's not too much oh no, he's sold plenty of fish and he has plenty of money in his pocket so they can eat smoked meat and roasted ham and dumplings and boiled peas and rutabaga and whatever they want for days and months in Matstova should they want to, Åsleik says, and he lifts his tankard to his mouth and drinks his beer and he wipes his mouth and he dries his beard and he breathes deeply in and out and then he looks at Alida and he asks why on earth things are so bad with her and she says no and they sit there in silence again and they begin to eat again and then Alida sips her beer and Åsleik says he has his boat moored at the Wharf and he's sailing northward tomorrow, he's sailing to Dylgja, he says, and does she want to come, and go back home again, she can do that, and if she doesn't have any other place to sleep tonight she can sleep on the bench in his cabin, Åsleik says, because there's a bench she can lie on there, and a bedspread to cover herself with, he can give her that, he says, and Alida looks at him and she doesn't know what to think or what to say and she doesn't know where to stay tonight here in Bjørgvin, and does she know what she'll do with herself if she goes to Dylgja, no she doesn't, because Pa Aslak won't be there and she doesn't want to go to her mother, she'll never set foot in Brotet again, no matter how bad it is with her and with little Sigvald, never that, no never that, Alida thinks, and she lifts the tankard and she sips the beer

Yes after such good and salty food you need lots to drink, Åsleik says

and he empties his tankard and he says that he wants to get a new one, and can he bring one for her too, but it looks like she has so much left that it can wait, he says

But as I said, you're welcome to sleep in my boat, he says

and they sit there in silence

It was sad about your mother, he says

About my mother, Alida says

Yes, yes that she should die so suddenly

and Alida flinches, not very noticeably, but she does flinch, so her mother's dead, she didn't know that, and it's all the same to her, she thinks, but it's sad too, Alida thinks and grief fills her and her eyes become wet

I was at her funeral, Åsleik says

and Alida covers her eyes with her hands and she thinks that now her mother is dead and it's all the same to her, but she mustn't think like that, for her mother is dead, she was her mother after all, no it's too awful, Alida thinks

What's wrong, Åsleik says

Are you thinking about your mother, he says

Yes, Alida says

Yes, it was sad that she should leave us so suddenly, he says

She wasn't all that old, he says

And not sickly either was she, he says

It's hard to understand, he says

and they sit there in silence for a long time and Alida
thinks that now that her mother's dead she can go back to
Dylgja, perhaps she can live in Brotet too, now that her
mother's dead, she thinks, for she has to find somewhere
to stay, she thinks, she must find somewhere for herself
and little Sigvald, she thinks

Well, you think about it, Åsleik says

Yes, if you want to come back to Dylgja, he says

and Alida sees Åsleik stand up and there's a bounce in
his step when he walks across the floor toward the counter
and Alida thinks that she and little Sigvald have to sleep
somewhere, for she is so tired, so tired, she could fall asleep
at once, sitting there on the chair, she thinks, and now that
her mother's gone she can go back home again can't she,
but it's terrible that her mother's dead, it's too sad and now
she's so tired, so tired, Alida thinks, because she's walked
and walked, that she has, first in from Stranda to Bjørgvin
and then all around the streets of Bjørgvin, she has walked
and walked and she has hardly slept, and she's been walking for so long, how long has it been since she has slept,
that she doesn't know, she has walked and walked and
looked for Asle, that's what she's done, but Asle isn't to be
found anywhere and how will she manage without him,
Alida thinks, and perhaps he's gone to Dylgja, Alida
thinks, he could've done that, but no, he wouldn't, not
without her, because Asle isn't like that, she knows that,
Alida thinks, but what has become of him, he was only
going to Bjørgvin to do a few errands, he said, and she saw
him standing there in the doorway, and didn't she feel then
that she would never see him again, yes she did, and she
asked him not to go, yes she did, but he said he had to go,
it didn't help what she said despite feeling in her whole

being that she would never see Asle again, but that, the
fact she felt like that, was perhaps just a feeling, that's what
she was thinking, again and again, but Asle didn't come
back, days passed by, and nights passed by, and Asle didn't
come back and she couldn't just sit there in the house,
without food, without anything at all and so she packed
everything they owned in two bundles and then she walked
to Bjørgvin, and it was a long walk, and it was heavy to
carry both the bundles and little Sigvald, and she had nothing to eat, and she found water in brooks and rivers, and
she walked and walked and ever since she arrived in
Bjørgvin she's been wandering the streets and searching for
Asle and sometimes she asked and then people just looked
at her and shook their heads and said something like
Bjørgvin is so full of guys like that and how could they
know who she's talking about, that's what they said, and
finally Alida was so tired that it felt as if she could no longer stand on her feet and her eyes fell shut again and again
and then she sat down with her back against the wall of a
shack on the Wharf in Bjørgvin and now she's sitting there
and has eaten the most wonderful food in the whole world
and she is so tired, so tired, Alida thinks, and here, here
it's nice and warm, she thinks, and her eyes fall shut and
then she sees Asle standing there in the doorway of the
house in Stranda saying that he won't be long, he's just got
an errand to do in Bjørgvin, he says, and then, as soon as
the errand is finished he'll come back to her, Asle says, and
she says he mustn't go, because then she might never see
him again, that's what it feels like, Alida says, and Asle says
that today is the day, today is when he's going to Bjørgvin,
but he'll come back to her as soon as he can, Asle says, and
then she hears Åsleik saying that now the tankard's full

again, and she opens her eyes and sees Åsleik put the tankard down on the table and he sits down and he looks
straight at Alida and he says that yes, as he said, if she has
nowhere else to go, she can sleep on his boat, as he said,
he says, and Alida looks at him and nods and then he lifts
his tankard and says let's drink to that, and Alida lifts her
tankard and then they clink and they toast each other and
both drink a little and then they sit there in silence, both
have eaten their fill, and both are tired and warm after all
the good food, and after the beer, and Åsleik says that he's
a bit sleepy now, he wouldn't mind a bit of a snooze, he
says, and the boat, well luckily it's right here on the Wharf,
not far to walk, so perhaps they should go aboard and get
some rest, at least an afternoon nap, Åsleik says, and Alida
says that she is very tired, she could fall asleep on the chair
she's sitting on, she says, and Åsleik says that they'd better
finish their drinks and then they can go and have a rest,
he says, and Alida says yes let's do that and she drinks a
little beer and she sees that Åsleik empties his tankard in
a couple of long swallows and then Alida says that he can
have the rest of her beer, if he wants it, she says, and then
Åsleik lifts her tankard, too, to his mouth, and he drinks
up the rest of the beer in one long swallow and then he
stands up and Alida puts little Sigvald to her breast and
then Åsleik lifts up the two bundles and then he begins to
walk toward the door and Alida walks after him and she
is so tired that she can barely stand on her feet and she
thinks that she just has to look at Åsleik's back, and her
eyes slide shut and then she sees Asle sitting there on the
chair and there's a wedding and he's playing and the music
lifts up and it lifts him and it lifts her and then they soar
together with the music, along in the thin air and they are

together like a bird and they are a wing each, and as one
they fly across the blue sky and everything is blue and light
and blue and white and Alida opens her eyes and she sees
Åsleik's back there ahead of her and she sees his cap pulled
down on his neck and he walks along the Wharf and Alida
stops and there, next to her foot, lies a bracelet, oh how
yellow and blue and how fine, she has never seen such a
nice bracelet, in the yellowest gold and with the bluest
pearls, Alida thinks, and she bends down and picks it up,
oh how nice, she has never seen anything so nice before,
how yellow and blue, she thinks, and then, imagine, imagine it lying there on the Wharf, and right next to her foot,
and she holds the bracelet up in front of her, and why was
the bracelet just lying there, she thinks, someone must've
lost it, she thinks, but now, now it's hers, now and forever
the yellow and blue bracelet will be hers, Alida thinks, and
she holds the bracelet in her free hand and it's unbelievable, she thinks, that someone could lose such a nice bracelet, that they could care so little about losing it, she thinks,
but now, now it's her bracelet, and she'll never lose it, Alida
thinks, because now she knows it, now she knows that it's
a gift to her from Asle, she thinks, but how can she think
like that, no she mustn't, she finds a bracelet on the Wharf
in Bjørgvin and she thinks it's a gift from Asle, but it is, the
bracelet is a gift to her from Asle, she just knows it, Alida
thinks, and never, never again, never again will she see Asle,
she thinks, that too she knows, Alida thinks, but she doesn't
know how and why she can know such things, she just
does, Alida thinks, and she sees that Åsleik is a fair bit
ahead of her on the Wharf and she sees that he stops and
looks at her and she slips on the yellow and blue bracelet,
imagine, imagine that she now owns such a nice bracelet,

the nicest bracelet in the world, Alida thinks, and she sees
that Åsleik has stopped and he points and says do you see
the headland over there, Pynten, they call it, that's where
they hang people, he says, and not long ago, just a couple
of days ago someone from Dylgja was hanged there, he
says, but that, I suppose you know that, he says, of course
you do, Åsleik says, because him, yes that Asle, you knew
him well, didn't you, he says, and Alida doesn't understand
what he means and he's still pointing, there, out there on
Pynten, Asle was hanged there, I saw it myself, I was there
and watched when he was hanged, as I was in Bjørgvin
then, Åsleik says, of course, he says, but you know that,
perhaps you were there too, he says, because isn't he the
father of your child, yes that's right, he says, that's what
they say at least, it's got to be him, right, Åsleik says, and
if you don't get away from Bjørgvin they'll hang you too,
he says, so now, now we'll get into my boat, he says, before
they take you and hang you too, Åsleik says, and Alida
hears what he says and she doesn't hear it and she's so tired
that she doesn't understand anything and Åsleik says it was
awful to see a fellow villager hanged, and then hanging
there with the rope around his neck, but if it was true what
they said, that he'd killed a person, at least one person,
then it was right, Åsleik says, and her mother, what
could've happened to her, he said, she died so suddenly,
and the next day both she and Asle were gone, why, and
the man who wanted to have his father's Boathouse back,
and who asked Asle to move, because that's how it had to
be, that's what they said at least, why was he found as a
corpse in the sea, drowned, how did that happen, he says,
but all this no one knew anything about for certain, but
it was different with an older midwife here in Bjørgvin,

there was no doubt in her case, she was killed, strangled, choked, no doubt there, they say, Åsleik says, and whoever does that, yes he deserves to be strung up and to die in front of a crowd of watching eyes, the way Asle died, he says, imagine doing something like that, Åsleik says, and Alida hears that he's talking and talking and she doesn't understand what he's saying and she sees Asle walking ahead of her along the Wharf and he's carrying the two bundles and then he says that they have to get out of Bjørgvin, they must keep going, and then they'll sit down and have a good long rest, and then they will have a good meal, he has managed to get a lot of good food, he says, and she looks at Åsleik's back and he walks along the Wharf and Alida holds her fingers tight around the yellow and blue bracelet, the nicest bracelet in the whole wide world, and she sees that Asle stops and he looks at her and when she has come to him, he says that they have to walk faster until they have gotten out of Bjørgvin, then they can slow down, then they'll have all the time in the world, then they can rest and eat and live a quiet life, Asle says, and he begins to walk again and Alida sees that Åsleik stops and he says there's my boat, a good little vessel, oh yes she is, Åsleik says, and Alida watches as he climbs aboard and he puts her bundles down on the deck and then Åsleik stands there and he stretches out his arms and she hands him little Sigvald while she squeezes the bracelet, the nicest bracelet in the whole wide world, so yellow and so blue, and Åsleik takes little Sigvald on his arm and they hear an angry scream and Alida doesn't take the hand Åsleik stretches out to her and she steps across the railing by herself and then she is aboard and she stands safely on deck and little Sigvald screams and cries and carries on and Åsleik hands

him to her and Alida holds him tight to her breast and
lulls him back and forth and little Sigvald stops his screaming and then he breathes calmly again against her breast

Yes, this is my vessel, Åsleik says

I fish, and I take the fish to Bjørgvin, he says

And now I've got plenty of money, he says

and he slaps his back pocket and Alida's eyes slide shut
and she sees Asle sitting there at the back of the boat holding the tiller and their eyes meet and it feels as if her eyes
are his and as if his eyes are hers and their eyes are as big
as the ocean, as big as the sky and she and he and the boat
are like a solitary shining movement in the shining sky

No you mustn't fall asleep now, Åsleik says

and Alida opens her eyes and the shining movement
disappears and becomes nothing and that was all and she
feels Åsleik's hand around her shoulder and he says that
it was a bad business with Asle, but of course it wasn't
her fault, nothing to do with her, he says, he too understands that much, but there could be people who believed
differently, so if she stays here in Bjørgvin she might be
suspected of having had something to do with it, that's
quite possible, he says, so he'd advise her not to stay here
in Bjørgvin, he says, but she's safe for now in his cabin,
Åsleik says, and he leads her along the deck and he says
that the barrel is here in the booth with a door behind the
cabin, after all they've been eating and drinking perhaps
she needs to know where the barrel is, he says, he needs
to visit the barrel himself now, he says, and he opens the
door to the cabin and he says here is my little home on
the sea, not too bad, if I say so myself, he says, and Åsleik
enters and he lights a lamp and Alida can only just see
in the half darkness that there is a bench and a table and

Åsleik says what a dreadful thing that Asle dragged her
into, he says, it's unbelievable, but now he has been pun-
ished, and that with a vengeance, he says, now he has paid
with his life, Åsleik says, and Alida can just see that there
is a bench and a table and a small stove she can see as well
and she sits down on the bench and she puts little Sigvald,
who is sleeping safely and soundly now, down against the
bulkhead and she squeezes the fine yellow and blue bracelet with her fingers, the finest bracelet in the whole wide
world, Alida thinks, and she sees Åsleik putting wood in
the oven

We'd better warm it up in here, he says

and Åsleik puts shavings and wood in the oven and he
lights it and it starts to burn right away and he says that
he's going to the barrel and he goes out and Alida holds the
bracelet up in front of her and how nice it is, she thinks,
how yellow and how blue and how nice, it must be of the
purest gold, and then these blue pearls, like the sky when
she and Asle were the sky, like the sea when she and Asle
were the sea, so yellow and so nice and so blue are the
stones, Alida thinks, and the bracelet is a gift from Asle,
she is sure of that, Alida thinks, she just knows it, she's as
sure as anyone can be, it's as certain as anything can be,
she thinks, and she fastens the bracelet around her wrist
and there it will stay from now on for as long as she lives,
Alida thinks, and she looks at the bracelet, oh how nice,
how very nice, she thinks, and her eyes fill with tears and
she is so tired so tired and she hears Asle saying that now
she will sleep, now she will rest for a long time, that's what
she needs, he says, and the bracelet, that's from him, he
says, he wants her to know that, even if she didn't get it
from him, that was impossible, but the bracelet is a gift

from him to her, he traveled to Bjørgvin, he says, to buy
rings for them, but then he saw this much too beautiful
bracelet and then all he could do was buy it, and now she
has it, even if she found the bracelet, it is from him, it's
his gift to her, Asle says, and then Alida lies down on the
bunk and she stretches out and she puts on the bracelet
and she hears Asle asking if she likes the bracelet and she
says that it's nice, it's the nicest bracelet she has ever seen,
she would never have believed there could be such a nice
bracelet in the whole world, so thank you, thank you from
all my heart, she says, he is so kind, her good boy, and
now, now she is all right, Asle says, and she says that she
has gone to bed now and she is going to sleep, and she has
a roof over her head, and it's warm here too, so everything
is well both with her and little Sigvald, she says, he doesn't
need to worry, everything's fine, everything's as fine as it
can be, Alida says, and then Asle says that she must sleep
well and Alida says that they will talk tomorrow and then
she feels herself sinking down into her tired body and then
she sees nothing and everything's dark and everything's soft
and dark and a little wet and Åsleik comes in and he looks
at her, and then he finds a blanket and covers her with it
and he puts more wood in the oven and he sits down at
the end of the bunk with his back resting against the bulkhead and he looks ahead and he smiles and then he turns
down the wick in the lamp and it gets dark and then he
lies down, fully clothed, on the deck and then everything
becomes silent and the only sound is the sea that pounds
lightly and sloshes against the side of the boat, the sloshing and then the light pounding in the boat and then the
crackling from the wood that has almost burned away and
Alida can feel Asle's arms around her and he's whispering

my dear one, my only one, you, you forever, Asle says, and
he holds her tight and he strokes her hair and then she
says you're my dear one forever, Alida says, and then she
hears the even breath of little Sigvald and then she hears
Asle's even breath and his warmth goes into her and then
she and he breathe evenly and everything is calm and then
there are calm movements and she and Asle move in the
same calm movements and everything is silent and blue
and unbelievable and Alida wakes up and she looks around
and where is she and it's rocking vigorously up and down,
and what's this, where is she, she thinks, and she sits up
in the bunk and she is in a boat and they are at sea, yes,
and yesterday she came aboard with Åsleik, because she
and little Sigvald had to sleep somewhere, and here she has
slept and now she is awake and little Sigvald is sleeping on
the bench there and she walked to Bjørgvin to find Asle,
but she didn't find him, and then she sat down and where
is she now, Alida thinks, where is she going, Alida thinks,
and she looks at the bracelet, oh how nice it is, and now,
yes now she remembers, yes that she found the bracelet
there on the Wharf, and how nice it is, how yellow, how
blue, and it was a gift from Asle, she thought that it was,
but it can't be, it must be a bracelet someone has lost, but
nice, yes it's nice, and now it's hers, and then Åsleik said
that her mother was dead, and that Asle was dead, that
they'd hanged him, and yes, yes that's how it is, and now
she's on Åsleik's boat and they're sailing toward Dylgja,
because she couldn't just stay there in Bjørgvin, she didn't
have a place to stay, she didn't have any money, and then
Åsleik said she could come back with him to Dylgja, and
so they're probably sailing there, Alida thinks, and since
she won't find Asle in Bjørgvin anyway, perhaps it's just

as well, she has to stay somewhere, little Sigvald has to stay somewhere, they can't be nowhere, and now that her mother's dead perhaps she can go back home and stay there, Alida thinks, but it did give her a little shock to hear that Asle's dead, that he was hanged, that he was hanged out there on Pynten, no, no Asle is alive, he must be alive, he's alive, of course Asle is alive, anything else is impossible, Alida thinks, and she stretches out and she sees little Sigvald lying there sleeping so safely and soundly and she opens the door and goes out and a fresh wind blows into her face and lifts her hair up and there's a good salty smell and she turns and there at the tiller she sees him whose name is Åsleik calling out good day good day, I can't say good morning because the day is too far advanced for that, Åsleik calls, and Alida looks around and she sees the sea out there, the open sea, and she sees the land in there, ridges and reefs, with no growth on them, just bare rock

We're making good speed, the wind's good, Åsleik says

And we've had a good tailwind all the way from Bjørgvin, he says

And we're approaching Dylgja, he says

and a powerful gust of wind grabbed the sails with a loud bang

There, hear that, he says

Oh yes, the wind's good, he says

So we'll arrive in Dylgja before too long, he says

We're approaching Dylgja, Alida says

Yes, Åsleik says

But what will I do there, she says

I thought, he says

You thought, she says

Yes that you yourself chose to come, Åsleik says

Yes, Alida says

Yes I thought it would be best for you to come to Dylgja, for where would you and your child go in Bjørgvin, he said

and Alida walks across the deck, and she stops next to Åsleik, steady on her sealegs

But I have nowhere to go in Dylgja either, she says

You've got your sister there, he says

But I don't want to go to her, Alida says

Why not, he says

and then they stand there without saying anything and the wind seizes the sails and their hair and now and then a wave rolls over the bow and across the deck

There's nothing for me in Dylgja, says Alida

Oh no, Åsleik says

You must put me ashore somewhere, she says

But what are you going to do there, he says

And what will I do in Dylgja, she says

and once again they stand there without saying anything

Yes, Åsleik says

and then he doesn't say anything else and then Alida doesn't say anything either

Yes, well my mother's dead, and I could use someone to keep house for me, Åsleik says then

and Alida just stands there without saying anything

You're not answering me, he says

I'm looking for Asle, she says

But he, yes I told you what happened to him, Åsleik says

and Alida hears what he says and she doesn't hear it, because of course Asle can be found, anything else is impossible, out of the question

Yes I told you yesterday what happened to him, Åsleik says

and it's not true, because it's just something he's saying, Alida thinks

Yes, that's what happened to him, Åsleik says

I saw it myself, he says

and they stand there in silence

I saw them hanging him and I saw him hanging there, he says

and Alida thinks that she and Asle are still sweethearts, they are with each other, he is with her, she with him, she in him, he in her, Alida thinks, and she looks out across the sea, and in the sky she sees Asle, she sees that the sky is Asle, and she notices the wind, and the wind is Asle, he is there, he is the wind, if he doesn't exist, he is still there and then she hears Asle saying that he is there, she sees him there, if she looks out across the sea she'll see that he is the sky she sees there above the sea, Asle says, and Alida looks and of course she sees Asle, but not just him, she sees herself too there in the sky and Asle says that he too exists in her and in little Sigvald and Alida says that yes he does, he always will and Alida thinks that now Asle is alive only in her and in little Sigvald, now she is Asle in life, Alida thinks, and then she hears Asle saying I am there, I am with you, I am always with you, so don't be afraid, I will follow you, Asle says, and Alida looks out to the sea and there, on the sky there, she sees his face, she sees it like an invisible sun, and then she sees his hand, it lifts up and it waves to her and Asle repeats that she must not be afraid and he says that she must take good care of herself and little Sigvald, she must look after herself and little Sigvald as best as she can, and then, before too long, then they'll

meet again before too long, Asle says, and Alida feels his
body close to hers and she feels his hand stroking her hair
and she strokes his hair

Yes so what do you say, Åsleik says

and Alida asks Asle what he means and he says if it's
best that she go with Åsleik, because where else will she
go, he says, then that's what's best both for her and for
little Sigvald

Keep house for you, Alida says

Yes, Åsleik says

And of course you'll have food and shelter for you and
the child, he says

Yes, Alida says

And pay, yes, more than other servant girls get, I promise you that, he says

and Alida hears Asle saying that it's probably for the
best, and he'll be with her, yes, he says, she mustn't be
afraid, he says, and then Asle says that they'll talk later and
Alida says yes they will

So what do you say, Åsleik says

and Alida doesn't answer

I live in Vika, you know, he says

There I have a house and a boathouse and a barn, he
says

And a good safe harbor, with a jetty, he says

And a few sheep, and a cow, he says

And I live there alone now, since my mother died, he
says

So what do you say, Åsleik says

You'll get both meat and fish, he says

And potatoes, he says

and Alida thinks where else could she go, and that

being a servant girl at Åsleik's is probably the best choice

Yes where else can I go, Alida says

So you're saying yes, Åsleik says

I suppose I am, she says

It'll be for the best, Alida says

Yes I'm sure it will, Åsleik says

Yes, I should say so, he says

I don't know what else I can do, she says

There, there, Åsleik says

I need a woman in the house, and you need somewhere to live, you and your child, he says

And it won't be long before we're there, he says

And Vika, it's a nice place, you'll find it a good place to live, he says

and Alida says that she needs to go to the john and Åsleik says that it's there, behind the door there, he says and points, there's the barrel, in the cubicle, he says, and Alida opens the door and she goes in and she fastens the hook and she sits down and then she sits there and it's good to sit there and do what she needs to do and good in any case to not have to do it outside, Alida thinks, and she doesn't understand much of what's happening any longer, she thinks, and she may as well be a servant at Åsleik's as anywhere else, he's probably no worse than anyone else, perhaps he's even better, that's possible, because she certainly won't go home to her sister in Brotet, how could she even have thought of that, because she did think, didn't she, that she could go to her sister and ask if she could live with her, how could she have thought of that, and it's much better to be a servant at Åsleik's, she'd much rather that, Alida thinks, so she might as well be a servant at Åsleik's, Alida thinks, because where else would she go,

now Asle is gone, and Asle is still with her, no, she doesn't
understand any of it, Alida thinks, and then she hears
Åsleik beginning to sing, I'm a sailor of life, he sings, the
boat is my world, I sail under the stars, I am close to the
sky, and the girl is my love, and the sea is my dream, I sail
under the stars with the moon my cocoon, he sings, and
he hasn't got much of a voice to sing with, Alida thinks,
but his voice sounds glad and happy, and it's good to hear
him sing, Alida thinks, and what did he say, cocoon, the
moon my cocoon, is that what he said, whatever could that
mean, Alida thinks, and she has done her business but she
keeps sitting there on the barrel, and cocoon, what could
that be, she thinks, and then she hears Åsleik calling have
you fallen asleep in there and she says no I haven't and he
says glad to hear it and then he asks if she has made up
her mind, yes, if she wants to be his serving girl and she
doesn't answer and he says that she has to make up her
mind soon, he says, because now he can see Storevarden
there on the headland, he says, and then they don't have far
to sail until they come to Vika, he says, and Alida stands
up and then she stands there and she hears Asle saying
that the best thing to do is to be a servant at Åsleik's and
Alida says that it probably is because where else could she
go, she says, and Asle says that they'll have to talk later,
she'll go home with Åsleik, she says, that's for the best and
then she lifts up the hook on the door and she walks out
into the fresh wind and then closes the door behind her
and fastens the hook on the outside of the door and then
she stands there holding herself steady and her long black
hair flutters in the wind and Åsleik looks straight at her
and asks what'll it be

    Yes, Alida says

What do you mean, Åsleik says

Yes I will work for you, she says

You will be my servant girl, he says

Yes, Alida says

and Åsleik lifts his hand and says look, look there, there's Storevarden, there on the headland, he says, and Alida sees a wide and tall beacon, rock laid upon rock, on a knoll on a long promontory and Åsleik says that yes, seeing Storevarden always fills him with joy because that means he's almost home again, he says, now they'll sail around the headland and then inward along the coast for a bit and then they'll be in Vika, he says, and when they've gone a bit further inward, she'll see the house she's going to live in now, Åsleik says, and she'll see the boathouse and the wharf, and she'll see the hills and fields and the whole glorious lot, he says, and since there are two of them on board now, it'd be good if she could help a bit and steer the boat while he's lowering the sails, so they can moor the boat in the best way possible, and Alida says she doesn't mind trying, but she has never steered a boat before, and Åsleik says come here and he'll show her, and Alida stands next to Åsleik and he says that she must take the tiller and then Alida stands and holds the tiller and can she try and change the course a little to port and she looks at him and he says that port is the same as left and Alida turns the tiller a little and Åsleik says that if it's going to make a difference, she'll have to turn it much harder and Alida does and then the boat glides a bit out to the sea and Åsleik says that now she can turn the tiller to starboard, which is right, he says, and Alida does that and then the boat drifts more toward land again and Åsleik says that now she must straighten out and Alida asks what he means by that and

Åsleik says that now she's going to sail straight ahead and she can aim for about ten meters outside the headland where Storevarden is and Alida understands that she will steer the boat toward that place and she turns the tiller a little back and then the boat drifts evenly forward and Åsleik says that they couldn't expect anyone to do better than that and when they've come around the headland she must take control, he says, and then he'll look after the sails, lower them, and then she must do exactly what he tells her, if he says a little to port, she must turn the tiller, but not a lot, and if he says hard to port, she must turn the tiller more forcefully, he says, and Alida says that she'll do that, she'll do exactly as he says as well as she can, she says, and Åsleik comes and takes over at the tiller and he looks at her bracelet

Well, what a nice bracelet, he says

Imagine you having such a nice bracelet, he says

and Alida looks at the bracelet, she had totally forgotten the bracelet, but how could she, she thinks, and it's so nice, she has never seen anything as nice, she thinks

Yes, Alida says

and they stand there without saying anything

That's strange, he says then

What, Alida says

Yesterday, before I saw you sitting there, yes, someone asked me if I'd seen a bracelet, he said

Yes in Bjørgvin you bump into all sorts of people, he says

Yes, Alida says

Yes, you know, she was that kind, Åsleik says

It was just before I met you, a bit further out on the Wharf, he says

Yes you can imagine what she wanted, he says

But I, yes I, he says

Yes you see, he says

Yes, she says

I thought she asked if I'd seen the bracelet just to get into a conversation, he says

And then, when I said, well you know, then she said she's lost a bracelet, such a nice bracelet, of the yellowest gold and with the bluest of blue pearls, he says

And then she asked if I'd seen it, he says

It's a bracelet that must look like the one you're wearing, he says

Yes, Alida says

Yes it must, he says

and Alida thinks that no, no it can't be this bracelet, because Asle has given her this bracelet, and Åsleik can say what he wants, but this bracelet was given to her by Asle, because Asle told her, Alida thinks, and she hears Asle telling her that this bracelet is my gift to you, he says, and the girl Åsleik is talking about, she stole it from him, Asle says, and then she lost it, and then Alida found it, that's how it is, that's how it should be, that's how he wants it to be, Asle says, and Alida says that she knows that's how it is, and now the bracelet is around her arm, and she'll take very good care of it, she says, she'll never lose the bracelet, she says, no never, she says, and she can never thank him enough for such a nice bracelet, Alida says

Look, there you can see Vika, Åsleik says

and Alida sees a wharf and a boathouse, and then a little cottage and a little barn, the cottage is the uppermost of the buildings, the barn is a little lower and off to the side

Yes, this is Vika, Åsleik says

This is my kingdom, he says

And isn't it nice here, he says

I think this is the nicest place on earth, he says

Always when I see the houses here at home I'm filled with such joy, he says

Yes, I'm finally back home again, he says

It's not big and grand, but it's home, he says

Here, here in Vika, here I was born and raised, and here I'll die, he says

It was my grandfather who came here first, he says

He cleared the land, and he built on it, he says

He came from one of the islands out to the west, he says

And then he managed to buy this piece of land, he says

And here he stayed, he says

And his name was Åsleik, just like mine, he says

And he married a girl from Dylgja, he says

And they had many children, and one of them, the oldest, was my father, he says

And he too married a girl from Dylgja, and then I was born, and then my three sisters, who are all married now, and each of them has settled on a different island out to the west, Åsleik says

and he says that he and his mother have lived alone for many years in Vika, until his mother died last winter and he found himself alone and only then did he understand how much his mother had done, and how difficult it would be to manage without her, without all her toiling and slogging, he says, it's only when something's gone that you know what you had, he says, yes, his mother had been good for him all his days, he says, but she was old, she was ailing, and then she finally died, he says

Yes well, he says

Yes, he says

and they stand there without saying anything

He needs help, he says

Yes, really, he says

and he says that he wants to thank Alida for agreeing to be a servant girl at his place, he truly wants to thank her for it, he says, but now, now she must take the tiller, because now the sails must be lowered and Alida takes over the tiller and then she sees Åsleik release one rope at great speed and then the other one and then he pulls the rope and the sail flutters

A little to port, he calls

and then he's on the other side of the boat and he pulls a rope and the sail flutters even more and it falls and part of the sail is now lying on the deck

Even more to port, Åsleik calls

and then the sail hangs straight down and in one bound Åsleik jumps over to the other side and he pulls ropes and banners, he says damn it, now it's hanging down, and he tears and pulls and swears and screams and the sail loosens and then the whole sail lies on the deck

A little further to port, toward the wharf, you see where that is, he says

and then he is over by the other sail and he loosens knots and he pulls and he jumps from side to side and he lowers the sail and now there's almost no sail left

A little more to port, he calls

A little more, he calls

and Alida thinks she can hear anger in his voice and then he comes running over the deck

Straighten up, damn it, he calls

and he grabs the tiller and straightens it up

Keep a steady course, damn it

and Åsleik sprints across the deck again and he lowers the sails fully

A little to port, not much, a little, he calls

and the boat drifts toward the wharf

A little to starboard, he calls

and the boat glides in along the wharf, and Åsleik stands in front of the bow with a rope and he throws the loop of the rope around a bollard on the wharf and he tightens the rope and fastens the boat and then he takes another rope and even if it's far from the side of the ship to the edge of the wharf, he climbs up on the edge of the boat and in one leap he's standing on the wharf and he fastens the rope around another bollard and then he pulls the boat into the wharf and then Åsleik is back on board

You were good, you were a good girl, it went well, he said

The wind was as it should be, and you did well, he says

I wouldn't have managed that on my own, he says

and Alida asks how he would have gotten the boat ashore

I'd have had to tow it, he says

I'd have had to row the boat into the wharf, he says

How, Alida says

Towed it with the small boat, rowed it in with the small boat, Åsleik says

and she can hear little Sigvald crying loudly, and perhaps he's been crying for a long time, and she just hasn't heard him crying, all the sounds of sails and ropes and whatever it's all called and Åsleik shouting have perhaps drowned out little Sigvald's crying, Alida thinks, and she goes into the cabin and there in the bunk lies little Sigvald, he's lying there screaming and he's shaking his head from side to side

I'm here now, don't cry, Alida says

My good boy, she says

Good boy, she says

And she lifts little Sigvald up and she holds him against her breast and she says can you hear me Asle, can you hear me Asle, she says, and then she hears Asle saying that he can hear her, he's always with her, he says, and Alida sits down and she takes out one breast and she puts little Sigvald to her breast and he suckles and suckles and Alida hears Asle saying that he was hungry, wasn't he, he says, yes, now little Sigvald feels good, he says, and Alida says that now, yes now she feels good too, she says, and you should be here now, she says, and Asle says that he is there, he is always there with her and he will always be there, he says, and Alida sees Åsleik standing in the doorway

Yes he must be fed, he says

That he must, Alida says

Certainly, he says

I'll begin carrying things up to the house, he says

I bought a great many things in Bjørgvin, he says

Salt and sugar and rusk, he says

And coffee, and other things I don't want to mention, he says

and Alida hears Asle saying that because he ended up the way he did, it was a good thing that she could now be a servant in Vika, so that both she and little Sigvald would have both food and shelter, he says, and Alida says that if that's what he thinks, yes, that's how it is then, she says, and little Sigvald stops suckling and just lies there and then Alida stands up and goes out on deck and she sees Åsleik walking up the steep hill toward the house with a box on each shoulder, and she sees that there are many such boxes there on the deck, and a few sacks, and she thinks that here, here in Vika, here in Vika on Dylgja is where she'll live, in Vika she and little Sigvald will stay and for how long no one can say, perhaps she'll stay in Vika the rest of her days, she thinks, and then she thinks that she's certain that's how it'll be, she'll live out her days here in Vika. And that'll have to be good enough, she thinks. You can live your life here too, she thinks. And Alida climbs over the railing and steps down onto the wharf and she sees there's a path up toward the cottage and she sees Åsleik opening the door in the front of the house and walking in and Alida begins to walk up the path and Åsleik comes out and he says that it's good to be back in his own house, good to see his own cottage again, even if it's small, he says, and then he comes walking down the path and he says that there's a lot to be carried up to the house, whenever he's in Bjørgvin he usually stocks up so it lasts for a long time, he says, and Alida walks up to the cottage and she goes inside and she sees a stove in the corner, a table with a few chairs, a bench against the wall, and then there's the loft, with a ladder going up, and then she sees a door, and that's probably to the kitchen, Alida thinks, and she goes and puts little Sigvald down on the bench, he's sleeping soundly now, and she walks over to one of the windows and she sees Åsleik walking up the ladder with a sack on his shoulder and she asks Asle if he has anything to say and he says that everything is as good as it can be and Alida feels that she's so tired, so tired, and she walks over to the bench and she sees little Sigvald lying there against the wall and she's so tired, so tired, so exceedingly tired, and why was she so tired now, it's because of it all, she thinks, walking to Bjørgvin, trudging through Bjørgvin's streets, sailing here, all of it together, she thinks, and Asle, that he's gone and still so near, all of it, all of it together, Alida thinks, and she lies down on the bench and closes her eyes and she's so tired, so tired, and then she sees Asle pull up there on the road ahead of her, and she's so tired, so tired, she almost falls asleep, and Asle stands there and they've been walking for a long time, it must be several hours since they last saw a house, and now Asle has stopped

There's a house, we'll go up there, he says

We must get some rest now, he says

Yes, yes I'm so tired and so hungry, Alida says

You can wait here, he says

and Asle puts down the bundles and then he walks up to the house and Alida sees him standing there in front of the door, knocking, and then he waits, and then he knocks again

No one's answering, Alida says

Doesn't look like anyone's home, Asle says

and he pulls the door and it's locked and Alida sees Asle step back and then run up and throw his shoulder against the door and it cracks and creaks and the door opens a little and then Alida sees Asle walk over to a tree and he pulls out his knife and he cuts off a branch and then he goes and sticks the branch into the gap in the door and it breaks and the door opens a little more and then he runs up again and knocks into the door and it opens and Asle falls in through the door and then Alida sees him standing in the doorway

Better come now, he says

and Alida is so tired, so tired, and she thinks that they

can't just take over a house and she sees Asle walking into
the house and she just stands there and then she sees Asle
coming out again

No one's living here and no one's been here for a long
time, he says

We can stay here, he says

Come on, he says

and Alida begins to walk up to the house

We're lucky, Asle says

and Alida comes to and she opens her eyes and she sees
that it's almost dark now in the cottage where she's lying
and she sees Åsleik standing in the middle of the room
like a dark shadow and she sees him taking his clothes
off and she closes her eyes and she hears Åsleik walking
across the floor and he covers her with a blanket and then
he lies down in the bed under the blanket and he puts his
arms around her and holds her tight and Alida thinks that
it has to be like that, yes of course, she thinks, and then
she thinks that it's Asle who's holding her, and then she
doesn't want to think any longer, she thinks, and she lies
very still and it's quite nice here in Vika, the house is not
all that big, but it's in a good location on a hillside, and
there are green hills around the house, and the barn lies
a little further down toward the sea, where the boathouse
is, and where the wharf is, and Åsleik's boat is moored at
the wharf, it's not all that bad here and now the sheep are
grazing and the cow is in her stall, and Åsleik has milked
her, there's milk next to the oven in the kitchen, he says,
and can she milk, yes, of course she can, but everything she
can't do that she needs to do, he'll teach her, everything she
can't do that he can and that could be useful, he'll teach
her, he says and she'll be well looked after here, he says,

because he will struggle and toil if it's up to him, and work, if there's anything he can do it's work, as long as he's alive and able she and her boy will have a good life, he says, and it doesn't hurt and surely she and her boy will have a good life, he says, and it doesn't hurt and it's quite nice too isn't it and out there is the sea and the waves and the ocean and the wind and the seagulls are screaming and everything will be fine he says and she doesn't want to listen to the screaming seagulls anymore and to what he's saying and the days pass and one day is like the next and the sheep and the cow and the fish and Ales is born and she is such a fine little girl and she gets hair and teeth and she smiles and laughs and little Sigvald who grows and becomes a big boy who's so like her father the way she remembers him, remembers his voice when he sang, and Åsleik who's fishing and sailing to Bjørgvin with his fish and who comes home again with sugar and salt and coffee and cloth and shoes and spirits and beer and salted meat and she makes potato dumplings and they cure and dry meat and fish and the years pass and Little Sister is born and she is so fair and her hair is so fine and one day is like the next and the morning is cold and the stove warms them up and spring comes with its light and its warmth and the summer with its burning sun, and winter with its darkness and its snow, and its rain, and then snow and more rain and Ales sees Alida standing there, she's really standing there, she stands there in the middle of her kitchen, in front of the window, old Alida stands there, and she can't be doing that, that's impossible, she can't just be standing there, she's long dead, and she's wearing that bracelet she always wore around her arm, the golden one with blue pearls, no this is not possible, Ales thinks, and she stands up and she opens the

kitchen door and she walks into the living room and closes
the door behind her and she sits down in her chair, puts
the blanket around her, pulls it close, and she looks at the
kitchen door and she sees the door open and she sees Alida
entering and she closes the kitchen door behind her and
then Alida stops there on the floor, in front of the window
in the living room, she stands there, and her mother can't
be doing that, Ales thinks, and she closes her eyes and she
sees Alida walking into the yard there in Vika, and she's
walking with her, holding her hand, and brother Sigvald
walks out with them, and they stand outside the cottage
and Ales sees Pa Åsleik come walking up the path from
the wharf, holding a fiddle case in his hand, and she sees
brother Sigvald running to meet Åsleik

Here, little bugger, here's a fiddle for you, Åsleik says

and he hands the fiddle case to Sigvald and he takes it
and stands quite calmly, holding the fiddle case

Couldn't have made less of a fuss, could you, Åsleik says

No, incredible how he's been pestering us so much
about getting him a fiddle, Alida says to Ales

Yes, after he heard that fiddler play, the one from an
island far out to the west, Ales says

Unbelievable, Alida says

And since then he's been spending time with him as
often as he can, Ales says

Yes, Alida says

Yes, he's a good fiddler, Alida says

Yes, I believe he is, Ales says

He plays well, Alida says

But, Ales says

Yes, Sigvald's father was a fiddler, Alida says

and almost interrupts her

And his grandfather, Ales says

Yes, yes, Alida says

and her voice is almost brusque, and then they see Åsleik turn and go down to the boat again and Sigvald comes toward them with the fiddle case, he puts it down on the ground, opens the case, and then he takes out the fiddle, holds it up in front of him, holds the fiddle up to them and from the boat, in the sunshine, Åsleik comes toward them, and he carries a box, he stops next to them

I've done plenty of shopping in Bjørgvin, he says

and I even got hold of a fiddle, would you believe, he says

and it's supposed to be an excellent fiddle, he says

I bought it from a fiddler who needed other things more than the fiddle, he says

But I paid him well for it, more than he asked, he says

I don't think I've ever seen a man so shaky, he says

and Alida asks if she can have a look at the fiddle, and Sigvald hands her the fiddle, and then she sees that the dragon head on the scroll is missing its nose

That's a good fiddle, I can see that, Alida says

and she hands Sigvald the fiddle, he puts it back in the case and stands next to them, and then he stands there with the fiddle case and Ales thinks that Sigvald, her good brother Sigvald, he became a fiddler, but not much else, he had a daughter, born out of wedlock, and his daughter apparently had a son, and his name was Jon, they said, and he's a fiddler too and he's published a book of poems, they say, well, people do all sorts of things, Ales thinks, and Sigvald just disappeared, and now he'd be so old that he'd be dead anyway, he just disappeared and was gone and was never heard of, Ales thinks, and why is Alida just standing there, standing there in her living room, in front of the window, she can't be doing that, why can't she just go away, if she doesn't want to go away there's nothing else for it then, Ales thinks, and she sees that Alida is still standing there in the middle of the floor, and she can't let her mother just stand there, because it's her living room, and why doesn't her mother go away, why doesn't her mother disappear, why is she just standing there, why isn't she moving, Ales thinks, and Alida can't just be standing there, because she is long dead and gone, Ales thinks, and should she dare to touch her mother, to feel if she is really there, she thinks, but she can't be there, her mother died many years ago, she walked into the sea, they said, but she had no idea what happened, and they say all sorts of things, and she wasn't able to go to her mother's funeral in Dylgja, she has often thought about that, that she wasn't at her mother's funeral, but it was a long way to go, and she had many children, and her husband was away fishing, so how could she have managed, and perhaps it's because she didn't go to her funeral that her mother's standing there now not wanting to leave her, but surely she can't say anything to her, she herself has often thought that if her mother really went into the sea she can't ask her about it, but the story is that her mother was found on the foreshore, she can't ask her about it, because she's not that far gone that she can sit here and talk to a person long dead, even if it's her own mother, no that's impossible, impossible, Ales thinks, and Alida looks at Ales and she thinks that she notices that she is there, of course she does, and perhaps she is tormenting her daughter by being there, and she doesn't want that, why would she want to torment her own daughter, she doesn't want to torment her own daughter at all, her, her good daughter, her oldest daughter, and the only one of her two dear daughters who was able to grow up and who had her own children and grandchildren and Ales stands up and she walks with short slow steps toward the front door, she opens the door and she walks into the hallway and Alida walks after her with short slow steps and she too walks into the hallway and Ales opens the front door and walks out and Alida walks out after her and then Ales walks along the road, because if Alida doesn't want to leave her house, then she'll have to do it, Ales thinks, nothing else she can do then, Ales thinks, and she walks down toward the sea, in the rain, down from the house in Vika, she stops and turns, she looks at the house and all she can see is something darker in the darkness, then she turns back again and keeps walking down, then she stops on the foreshore, she hears the waves rolling and she feels the rain against her hair, against her face, and then she walks out into the waves and all the coldness is warmth, all the sea is Asle and she walks further out and then Asle is around her just like he was the night they first met when he played at the dance for the first time there in Dylgja and everything is only Asle and Alida and then the waves are rolling over Alida and Ales walks into the waves, she keeps walking, she walks out and out into the waves and then a wave rolls over her gray hair

Born in 1959 in Strandebarm, in Vestland, western Norway, **Jon Fosse's** remarkably prolific career began in 1983 with his first novel, *Red, Black*, and since then he has published numerous novels, stories, books of poetry, children's books, and essay collections. He began writing plays in 1993, with *Someone Is Going to Come*, and since then he has written almost thirty plays, including *A Summer's Day*, *Dream of Autumn*, *Death Variations*, *Sleep*, and *I Am the Wind*.

Since the mid-nineties his plays have had unparalleled international success, being performed over a thousand times all over the world; his works have been translated into more than fifty languages. Today Fosse is one of the most performed living playwrights, but he has continued to write novels, stories, and poetry of exceptional quality. In 2015, he received the Nordic Council Literature Prize for his work *Trilogy*, consisting of *Wakefulness*, *Olav's Dreams*, and *Weariness*. Fosse's earlier novels *Melancholy I* and *II*, *Morning and Evening*, and *Aliss at the Fire* have also received wide critical acclaim.

Dr. May-Brit Akerholt has extensive experience as a translator and production dramaturg of classic and contemporary plays. More than twenty of her translations have been produced by leading theatre companies around Australia and overseas. Her published translations include several plays by Ibsen and Strindberg; four volumes of plays by Jon Fosse (Oberon Books, London); three novels by Jon Fosse: *The Boathouse*, *Trilogy*, and *Essays* (all by Dalkey Archive Press). She has written a book on Patrick White's drama and a number of her critical articles have been published in various books and journals.

Dalkey Archive Essentials

Printed in the USA
CPSIA information can be obtained
at www.ICGtesting.com
JSHW021929181023
50413JS00003B/5

9 781628 973907